MASTER OF
THE OUTBACK

MASTER OF
THE OUTBACK

BY

MARGARET WAY

MILLS
BOON

First published in Great Britain 2012
by Mills & Boon, an imprint of Harlequin (UK) Limited.
Large Print edition 2012
Harlequin (UK) Limited, Eton House,
18-24 Paradise Road, Richmond, Surrey TW9 1SR

© Margaret Way, Pty., Ltd 2012

ISBN: 978 0 263 22578 5

Harlequin (UK) policy is to use papers that are natural,
renewable and recyclable products and made from
wood grown in sustainable forests. The logging and
manufacturing process conform to the legal environmental
regulations of the country of origin.

Printed and bound in Great Britain
by CPI Antony Rowe, Chippenham, Wiltshire

CHAPTER ONE

IT WAS spring. Regeneration was in the air. Parks and gardens across the city were aglow with dazzlingly beautiful massed displays of azaleas, rhododendrons, and an astonishing number of spring-flowering bulbs—gorgeous oriental lilies, iris, hyacinth, heavily scented freesias and jonquils, golden daffodils. Sensual perfumes hung over the city like a bride's fine tulle veil. The sky had the blue lustre of an opal, and a few puffy white clouds raced on high.

Genevieve Grenville was near skipping along herself, since the current of her life had picked up. It wasn't all that long ago since she had found herself at a very low point in her life. But that had been *then*. This was *now*—the future. Being positive, counting your blessings was the key. Move on and lock down the humiliating past. Pretty soon she just might be able to.

Her career was helping enormously. She was now a published writer, with a bestseller under her belt. She was certain her literary agent and editor, good friend Maggie McGuire, would have approved the final draft of her new book, *Lovers and Losers*. She was deeply indebted to Maggie for her belief in her, and her expert guidance. Maggie had been with her every step of the way. That included the woeful state of her private life that had left her wondering why she had any ego left.

Her debut novel, *Secrets of the Past*, had saved her, buoying her up. The hardback was doing a celebratory jig in her tote bag as she strode along, fired up with energy. It was a tremendous confidence booster to know that at twenty-seven she was making a name for herself in the literary world. When one was on a roll one had to stick with it; hence *Lovers and Losers* as her quick follow-up.

The reviews for *Secrets of the Past* had been thrillingly good… "A first-rate literary debut…" "A bright new star has appeared on the horizon…" Couldn't beat that. Even more gratifying was the incoming feedback from her readers. One couldn't be a successful writer without one's readership. She had encountered many of her readers wanting to express their appreciation. It was always a pleasure, even a humbling experience, when someone mentioned that reading her book had helped them through a small crisis or a bad patch in their lives.

Genevieve knew all about bad patches.

Secrets of the Past had even made an impact sufficient to carry a well-known magazine's gold sticker: GREAT READ. What better plug could she want? It had come at exactly the right time.

Her ex-fiancé, Mark Reed—the man she had entrusted with her life's happiness—had given in to temptation and slept with the young woman most off-limits in the world to him: her stepsister Carrie-Anne. Carrie-Anne was to have been her chief bridesmaid, for God's sake! She and Mark had been practically at the altar. She didn't think she would ever get over the treachery. The pain of betrayal still burned in her breast. Nor could she entirely control the image of the two of them naked in bed. They had taken something from her she would never get back.

Trust.

But she was over the worst of it. Stiff upper lip and all that. Writing was her solace. She had learned that living with pain, setbacks, and dis-appointments was what life was all about. If she had been less trusting she would have recognised pocket-size blonde Carrie-Anne's destructive potential. She had always been a devious little creature.

Mark's excuse took the cake. *"It was a moment of madness, Gena. It's you I love. But Carrie-Anne is always trying to get one up on you. It's your own fault, in a way. You didn't make enough time for me. Always the damned book!"*

What a cop-out! She *had* always made time for him, but she accepted the fact that spoilt rotten Mark had really wanted a woman like Mum, who spoke like a character in a Victorian novel and lived her life dancing attendance on her husband and her adored only son. Mrs Reed had once referred to it as a "noble sacrifice".

"Just hormones, Gena." That had been Carrie-Anne's excuse, her delicious little face contorted by crippling remorse. *"Hormones. They're so dangerous!"*

"Try sky-diving." Genevieve had advised caustically. *"Without a parachute. Better yet, take Mark."*

There were no excuses for despicable behaviour.

Her appointment with Maggie was scheduled for three o'clock. She had never been known to arrive late. When she did arrive there were two hopefuls waiting. Going to Maggie's was much like going to the doctor's. One could be assured of a wait. Maggie's receptionist Rhoda, a large, flat-faced woman, darted a disapproving glance in her direction. She might have been a full thirty minutes late, or committed the cardinal sin of turning up without an appointment.

"Good afternoon, Rhoda." Genevieve gave the dragon lady a brilliant smile.

Rhoda did not respond. No surprise there. But she did condescend to point a finger at a seat. Here was a woman who wouldn't win any votes for Receptionist of the Year.

With a smile and a nod to the other two hopefuls, Genevieve found a seat on the other side of the room, so she could take out *Secrets of the Past* and appreciate it all over again. She liked the cover. It depicted a beautiful young woman's downbent face above her pen-name: Michelle Laurent. It was the maiden name of her French-born paternal grandmother. "Michelle Laurent" was set in large letters *above* the title. So much better to have it above than beneath. Such an attractive-looking book would draw attention. She had seen it prominently displayed in a bookshop inside a major shopping mall she had cut through on her way over to Maggie's.

Secrets of the Past had been written at night, when she'd still been teaching English and French at her old Alma Mater—a prestigious college for girls. She had enjoyed her years of teaching since university, but as soon as her writing career had taken off she'd found herself in the enviable position of being able to write full-time. Her beloved Michelle's handsome legacy had made that possible.

Grandmère Michelle had started to teach her French at toddler stage. She had always given love, support and endless encouragement. To Genevieve's grief Michelle had died very suddenly of complications following a severe bout of influenza. That had been a short time before the manuscript for *Secrets of the Past* had been completed. It was balm to know Michelle had pored over its drafts and offered valuable insights, which Genevieve had wisely acted upon. Maggie often said Michelle was a better editor than she was—and Maggie was the best.

Genevieve had fully intended using her own name, but that all had changed when Michelle died. To her readership she was Michelle Laurent.

A tribute to her beloved grandmother. Her father had entrusted her to Michelle after her mother Celine had been killed in a catastrophic five-car pile-up on the freeway. Genevieve had been ten at the time. Her devastated father had taken a few years before remarrying the divorced socialite Sable Carville. Sable had brought her glamorous, much-photographed self to the marriage, along with her little girl, the adorable Shirley Temple look-alike Carrie-Anne, who soon took her step-father's surname Grenville.

So there they had been—the two little Grenville girls, Genevieve and Carrie-Anne. One tall for her age and gawky to boot, with an unmanage-able mane of red hair and freckles, the other the adorable Carrie-Anne, always exquisitely turned out by her fashion-plate mother. Genevieve hadn't received the same attention. Not much point spending time on a stepdaughter who didn't fit the description of "pretty". Only her father, a blue chip lawyer, had foreseen the day when the awkward cygnet would turn into a swan like her mother.

Her maternal grandparents were seldom in the country. After the death of their beloved only child they had become world-travellers, never staying anywhere for long. In their own way they were on the run from the tragedy, and from other family tragedies that reached back decades.

A very intense young man with a mop of bushy hair was being ushered out through Maggie's door, shaking his head in disbelief. From the expression of confusion and outrage on his face, he had discovered his prized manuscript *hadn't* been short-listed for the Booker Prize.

Maggie saw him off with an encouraging, "Keep at it, Colin." It was like a benign pat on the head. One of the other hopefuls spluttered into laughter. That was a bit unkind. Maggie jiggled her fingers at the two waiting hopefuls, and then gave Genevieve a big smile. "Come on in, Gena."

Genevieve gathered up her tote bag.

Maggie's office was very spacious, attesting to her success. The floor was carpeted wall to wall in neutral beige, with a luxurious oriental rug. Her desk was substantial—mahogany with curved legs. Two cream leather armchairs were placed in front of it, and there was a separate seating area with a sofa and armchairs grouped around a glass-topped coffee table. Three of the walls were lined with floor-to-ceiling bookcases filled with a lot of leather-bound books with gold lettering on their spines. A large portrait of a very handsome man took pride of place directly behind Maggie—looking over her shoulder, as it were. Most people were allowed to believe it was a family portrait, but Maggie had confessed after a drink or two that she'd bought it because it looked like Sir Richard Hadlee, the famous New Zealand cricket player, in his prime. Maggie had made Genevieve promise not to tell anyone.

Waving a hand towards some point on the ceiling, Maggie moved behind her desk. It was littered with so many manuscripts Genevieve always wondered how Maggie could work in such a shambles. Genevieve took a seat, depositing her tote bag on the floor.

Maggie reached for the glasses she was too vain to wear in public. "We've got a cracker here, Gena." She slapped a satisfied hand on top of the thick manuscript. "I thoroughly enjoyed it. Your readers will too. A stirring tale—great romance, extremely touching in places, all those amazing insights, and your usual clever twists."

Genevieve's heart lifted. "I'm glad you like it, Maggie. I owe a lot to you."

"Maybe a bit," Maggie conceded. "But you're a born writer."

"I've always had a compulsion to write going back to my childhood."

"Of course, dear—a prerequisite." Maggie looked up to smile. Maggie smiled often—unlike Rhoda. "So what next?" Maggie asked.

Genevieve shifted back in her chair "I think I'll take a break, Maggie. A complete change of scene—maybe six months or so. I've been going at it pretty intensively, as you know. Losing my grandmother hit me very hard, and then there was the debacle of my engagement."

"You're well rid of him," Maggie huffed. Maggie never kept her strong opinions to herself. "So he was a good-looking charmer? He turned out to be a traitor. As for that treacherous creature Carrie-Anne!" Maggie threw up her hands in disgust.

"I'm over it, Maggie," Genevieve said. Well, not completely. A *double* betrayal was hard to take.

"As I've told you before, dear, you've had a lucky break. Think—it could have happened after you were married. He could have betrayed you zillions of times over a lifetime. Honest to God, it brings tears to my eyes. Success puts men off, you know, love," she confided for the umpteenth time. "*I* should know."

Maggie had been twice married, twice divorced. Now she was eyeing Genevieve speculatively across the table, her pearly white teeth—the result of expensive cosmetic work—sinking into her bottom lip.

"You wouldn't consider a break in our fabled Outback, would you?" She asked on the off-chance, with no real expectation of Gena's saying yes. "You'd be staying on a famous cattle station in the Channel Country. It's owned and run by one of our most prominent landed families. I can line someone else up, but I thought you could handle it. Have a well-earned holiday as well—recharge the batteries, maybe get inspiration?

Out of nowhere Genevieve experienced one of those moments of searing awareness that came like a thunderclap. She didn't understand what prompted these moments, but she had come to think of them as a window opening up in her mind.

"What are we talking about here, Maggie? A working holiday?" Her voice sounded calm, but there was a betraying tension in her face.

Maggie's alert brown eyes sharpened. She

hadn't missed a bit of it, though she pretended not to notice. "That's it exactly." Maggie could sense Gena's inner disturbance, even if there didn't appear to be any apparent reason for it. "If you're interested, of course, Gena. Should be a piece of cake for you, with the bonus of an Outback holiday."

"More information?" Genevieve requested, knowing in advance what Maggie was going to say. It had been long recognised by the family that Michelle had had an extra sense. *She* had inherited it. No denying genetics.

"Of course, dear." Maggie lowered her eyes, giving Gena a little time to gather herself from that all too brief moment of—what, exactly? "A senior member of the family—Trevelyan is the name, *Miss* Hester Trevelyan, who's had the sense to avoid marriage—needs a ghost writer to help with the family history. That would be from colonial days. And she might want to bring in their illustrious Cornish family background. Richard Trevelyan emigrated to the free colony of South Australia in the mid-1800s. We know there was a big influx of Cornish migrants from the mid-nineteenth century right up until after

World War II. It was actively encouraged by the government, I believe."

Genevieve made a real effort to calm her agitation. "After the demise of their tin and copper mines. Cornish mines were known to traders as far back as ancient Greece. It was thought that with their wealth of experience and expertise Australia was the place to come for mining families. The New World—a new beginning. We still refer to Yorke Peninsula in South Australia as 'Little Cornwall'."

"So we do!" Maggie exclaimed. "These Trevelyans have their own family crest."

"How very jolly!"

"The Cornish side of the family did own tin and copper mines, as far as I know, but Richard Trevelyan was the last in a line of sons. He wanted to make his own way, so he decided to found his own dynasty in Australia. Apparently he was more interested in sheep and cattle than in getting involved in the mines—though I believe the Trevelyans *are* heavily involved in the mining industry. Also real estate, hotels, air, rail, and road freight. You name it. A lot of diversification going on there. The current cattle baron is Miss Trevelyan's great-nephew, Bret Trevelyan.

Bret short for Bretton, I guess. Bit of information on him: he's just thirty, still unmarried, one of the most eligible bachelors in the country. He was once engaged to the daughter of another well-heeled landed family, the Rawleighs. Obviously the grand romance and the unification of two dynasties fell through. His parents divorced when he was in his early teens. An acrimonious split, I believe. The mother ran off with a family friend—*tsk, tsk*. The father never remarried. He was killed in a bizarre shooting accident on the station. Apparently a guest's rifle discharged when he was climbing over a fence. I don't know the full story. There's a younger brother, Derryl, and a sister, Romayne. Romayne married the Ormond shipping heir two years back—remember? It was a big society wedding. Got a lot of coverage."

"I remember." Genevieve sat quietly. She knew all about the Trevelyan family.

"The cattle station is vast—on the Simpson Desert fringe," Maggie continued. "Djangala, they call it. Aboriginal. No idea what it means. You don't pronounce the D. They also own a chain of cattle *and* sheep stations across Queensland, New South Wales, the Northern Territory and the Kimberley. So they're super-rich and very proud of their heritage." Maggie sat back, intrigued by Gena's initial reaction. It was almost as though she had thrown a switch. "Miss Trevelyan is well into her seventies, but apparently still in good health."

Genevieve concentrated on breathing in and out gently. She hoped she didn't look as perturbed as she felt.

She had first overheard the name Trevelyan in a conversation between her maternal grandparents when she was twelve. Her grandparents had returned home on one of their periodic visits to celebrate her birthday. She had been about to enter the room to tell them lunch was ready when she was stopped in her tracks by the sound of her grandmother's voice. It had literally throbbed with pain. Even at that tender age she had known the pain sprang from a deep well of anguish—as if the event Nan spoke of had straddled her life and caused her the deepest torment.

Genevieve had since come to realise what was the past for some people was as yesterday to others.

Nan had been speaking of a tragic event in her youth, the trauma of it still fresh in her mind. Genevieve had hung back, a strange jangling in her ears. She hadn't been deliberately eavesdropping. She couldn't have moved even if she had wanted to. One peek had revealed tears pouring down her grandmother's face. The grief she'd suddenly felt had—incredibly—been a variation on Nan's own.

Afterwards, she hadn't dared ask who the Trevelyans were. She'd had to find out for herself years later. She wasn't about to tell Maggie the story now. She would be agog. But Genevieve knew beyond doubt that she would take on the role of ghostwriter for Hester Trevelyan. It was the only opportunity she would ever get.

CHAPTER TWO

Two weeks later.

HER nightmares came for her by night. Unlike most dreams, they didn't vanish on awakening; they stayed with her. She knew what caused them. The shock entry of the Trevelyans into her life.

Her maternal grandmother's first cousin, Catherine Lytton, had died in tragic circumstances on the Trevelyan family's Djangala Station in the late 1950s. It reassured Genevieve to know any family connection of hers would be difficult to trace. She wrote under the pen-name Michelle Laurent, and she was going to Djangala as Genevieve Grenville. She had insisted Maggie did not mention her blossoming literary career, let alone her pen-name. Maggie hadn't been altogether happy about it, but had given in to Genevieve's adamant request. It was essential she go incognito. Everything was organised for her trip.

Djangala had escaped being contaminated by scandal. Catherine's death had been deemed a tragic accident. A city girl, she had stepped too close to the crumbling edge of an escarpment the better to admire the stupendous view. The ground had abruptly crumbled beneath her, hurtling her to her death on the plain below. The Trevelyans and the police officer who had headed the investigation had been in total agreement—an accidental death that had devastated them all. A beautiful young woman with her whole life before her!

Not a word of the marriage proposal Catherine Lytton had received from Geraint Trevelyan ever surfaced. Only Catherine had written ecstatically about it to her favourite cousin.

Trevelyan had later gone on to marry Patricia Newell, long stuck in the wings as his future wife. Catherine had been on Djangala as companion for her friend Patricia. The two young women had gone to boarding school together and had kept up their friendship.

Once again the wheels of fate were set in motion.

Geraint Trevelyan was Bret Trevelyan's grandfather.

Genevieve's father, who had torn strips off Mark and Carrie-Anne, had given his approval of her new assignment, thinking it would hasten the healing process and that the Trevelyans were a splendid pioneering dynasty. He had no idea of Genevieve's true motivation. The Grenville side of the family had never learned Nan's secret. But Genevieve, given such an unforeseen opportunity, was determined on learning the truth about the final days of Catherine's life. She'd had a *burning* curiosity since the age of twelve—both because she was family and, it had to be said, due to her nature as a budding writer—to solve this mystery. Mysteries cried out to be solved.

Had Catherine's death simply been a disastrous accident? Or was there more to it? Had the Trevelyan family buried the truth, as Catherine's family had had to bury her broken body? The "accident" might well have revolved around the eternal triangle. People did terrible things for love.

Old faded photographs of the two young women revealed they had been physical opposites. Catherine tallish, very slender, with strawberry blonde hair, deep blue eyes and porcelain skin; Patricia petite, a little on the stocky side, with fine dark eyes and an abundance of dark hair. The photographs, all of them taken between the ages of sixteen and twenty-two, showed two young and untested girls.

* * *

Derryl Trevelyan, the younger son, was picking her up at her front door. They were to drive to the commercial airfield when the Trevelyan King Air was on standby to fly them to Djangala.

It was almost time to leave. She took one last look in the pier mirror.

Portrait of a serious-minded, bookish young woman, capable of taking on a challenge with no thought whatsoever of being on the lookout for an Outback millionaire.

Maggie had allowed her to read Miss Trevelyan's curt letter.

Please don't send me some glamorous young woman. Someone imagining she's going to have a good time along the way. Such young women annoy me. I want someone dedicated, serious about their work. I will possibly keep odd hours, depending on my health. There will be free time, but this is first and foremost a *job*. Not an Outback holiday. I don't need anyone, either, who will run off home when she realises just how isolated we are. A plain young woman would suit, as long as she's not dull and she knows what she's about.

Given such parameters, Genevieve had deliberately played down her looks. Her Titian mane
was drawn back tightly from her face and pinned
into a thick coil at her nape. She wore the lightest
make-up. She wore a silk shirt, but the colour was
a subdued chocolate, and not her usual skinny
jeans, but comfortable tan trousers and tan boots.
To further enhance the scholarly look she'd had
clear glass put into bookish frames.

She would have laughed at herself, only she felt
anything but lighthearted. She was going into the
Trevelyan desert stronghold where Catherine had
been trapped.

A young man struck a languid pose against the
passenger side of a late model hire-car. He was
wearing casual clothes, but managed to look the
very picture of sartorial elegance.

"Ms Grenville?" He looked her over. No smile.
Clearly she was a big disappointment.

"That's right," she responded pleasantly. "Would
you mind giving me a hand with my luggage?"

A slight hesitation, as though he was above such
things. "Certainly."

She was grateful for that small mercy. Taking
charge of the smaller suitcase herself, she pushed
the large suitcase through the front gate.

"That the lot?" he asked, as though his back had seized up.

"It's not exactly a *lot*." For the first time she looked directly into his face. He was handsome. Thick dark hair, clear tanned skin, eyes neither brown nor green but a mix of the two. "If I need anything else it can be sent on."

"Nice place you've got there." He was looking back at her contemporary single-storey home. It had great street appeal. She had lived in it, furnished to her tastes, for the past three years. Her father had given her the substantial deposit. He would have bought the house for her but she had insisted she pay it off. "Is it yours?" he asked, as though she were renting.

"It will be when I pay it off," she answered dryly.

During the drive to the airport he made little attempt at conversation. He did, however, deign to ask what she did.

"I'm a schoolteacher."

"Schoolteacher, eh?" He made it sound jaw-crackingly dreary.

"Well, up until fairly recently. I enjoyed teaching, but now I want to concentrate on my writing."

"That won't bring you in much," he commented, with droll disdain.

"Perhaps not." She was struck by his young-man arrogance. "And what about you? You're a cattleman?" He didn't look it. He might have been a male model. He didn't look *tough* either, in the way she imagined a man of the land would look.

"Bret's the cattle baron," he offered, all sarcasm now. "I'm the second son—the off-sider."

He made it sound like a drop-out. "Does that bother you?"

He shot her a sharp sideways glance, as if reassessing her. "I wouldn't change *my* life. Bret is the boss. I lag a long way behind. I wouldn't want the job anyway."

Most probably he couldn't handle it.

"Too much hard work, too much responsibility. No down-time. We all know all work and no play makes for a dull guy. I wouldn't want to handle the business side of things either. Bret is the brain."

Which let him off the hook. His brother Bret wasn't a dull guy, Genevieve was prepared to bet. Despite Derryl's claim he didn't want the job, and his feigned nonchalance, she had an intuitive grasp on the nature of the brothers' relationship.

Bret Trevelyan would be the *strong* one—Master of Djangala.

"And you have a sister? Romayne?" She got off what she recognised as a touchy subject. "Such a beautiful name. One doesn't hear it often."

"Ah, I see you've read up on us."

"A little. I *am* coming to live on the station for some months."

"Working for dear Aunt Hester." Sardonic emphasis on the *dear*. "She's got it into her head she wants a history of the Trevelyan family. Only problem is she's not a writer. That's where you come in. She used to be a very good pianist. Studied here and in London. Can't play now, which I count as a blessing. She used to go on and on for hours. Mercifully she has arthritis in her hands."

"That's a shame," Genevieve said with genuine sympathy. "Her playing would have given her great pleasure and comfort. Music has such power to soothe. You're fond of your great-aunt?"

He gave a theatrical sigh. "Impossible! Aunt Hester is a real old tartar. I'm not surprised no one wanted to marry her, for all the dowry she could have brought to a match. You'd think she was the Grand Duchess Anastasia, the way she acts. The only one she loves and listens to is Bret. He'll get her money as well—not that he needs it." His tone couldn't conceal a raft of hidden resentments.

She knew she was deliberately trying to draw him out. "Surely she loves you and your sister?"

"Yes. Romayne's married. Happily, thank God. Not much happiness in our family. Aunt Hester never took any notice of Romayne and me. Romayne is the image of our mother. Know about her?"

She answered with care. "Not really, Derryl. I know your father is dead. I know your parents were divorced. Is that right?"

He shrugged a shoulder. "You're going to hear it anyway. A pretty shabby affair, but it happens— even with royalty. Mother ran off with a family friend. Apparently she longed for a different life. Our father got custody. Our mother allegedly begged for Romayne, her girl. Dad told her to push off. There was no question of Bret's going to live with her. Bretton was the heir. Our father's longed-for Number One Son. Even as a kid Bret knew what his life was going to be. His destiny, if you like."

"You don't sound all that happy with *your* lot, Derryl?"

His answer was a curl of the lip. "Not so easy to

get away. Bret holds the purse-strings. He administers the family trust. Sometimes I feel trapped in a wasteland. At least Bret sent Romayne off with a splendid dowry, just like in the olden days. Not that her husband can ever get his hands on it. Bret saw to that. Romayne is financially secure for life, no matter what. Needless to say she worships the ground Bret treads upon."

To inspire such love Bret Trevelyan couldn't be all that bad, Genevieve thought. She shifted the conversation on to more general topics. Derryl evidently liked wallowing in self-pity.

Even at a distance, Bret Trevelyan radiated a powerful charisma. He broke away from a small all-male group as they pulled up, coming towards them. He was tall, very lean, but powerfully built, with straight wide shoulders and a body naturally endowed with virile grace. The group of cattlemen stood beside a very impressive twin turboprop she recognised as a Beechcraft King Air. One of her father's most important clients was a retail magnate who had recently bought the eight-seater, and employed a regular pilot. The Trevelyans' little run-about had cost *millions*.

That wasn't fair. She knew the King Air was the

toughest aircraft in its class. It could take off from both major airports and short gravelled runways, which would be a big plus in the Outback. There was another important factor: it could operate effortlessly at high altitudes and under extreme weather conditions, which it no doubt would encounter.

Up close, the Trevelyan lineage was apparent in both brothers. Only Bret Trevelyan appeared to be a man of a higher order. It was in the way he held himself, the way he moved. Indeed, it was hard to take her eyes off the man. She found him to be wonderful-looking. He had such an air of authority, such presence. Moreover, he had all the *toughness* she had found wanting in his younger brother.

"Ms Grenville?"

There was total composure in his voice, a self-assurance that would instantly inspire great confidence in *him*. He was inches taller than his brother—well over six feet. More disturbingly, he was looking down at her with the most brilliant dark eyes she had ever seen. She was someone who looked at eyes first. *His* eyes were so dark they were almost black, his gaze so powerfully searching she had the unnerving notion he was able to see right through her. In which case she might be sent packing. Only just thirty, he was an arrestingly handsome man, with an elegance about him and more than a touch of sensuality in the chiselled mouth and the strong, perfectly balanced bone structure. The air of command was that of a much older man. One seldom saw it in one so young, unless he was a truly exceptional person.

It came as a complete shock to realise she was attracted to him—and all in a matter of moments. That couldn't be. It rendered her vulnerable. On the reverse side of instant attraction lay the abyss. Catherine had found that out, if her claim of a serious love affair with Geraint Trevelyan were true. And why would it not be? Catherine hadn't lied.

She paused briefly to collect herself. "Genevieve, please. Or Gena, if you prefer."

They had extended hands at much the same time. Now a chain of little tremors ran down her spine as his long callus-tipped fingers fell over the soft skin at the back of her hand. Contact sparked a reaction akin to an electric thrill. She certainly felt a tingling right up her arm, and an odd thump of her heart. It was an extraordinary feeling, but nothing could be served by it. Whatever a woman felt for this man, she would just know it would be fathoms deeper than anything she had hitherto experienced.

"Genevieve it is." His brilliant eyes appeared to glitter for a single moment. Deeper, darker-toned than his brother's, his voice was similarly cultured. No ordinary "bushies" the Trevelyans. "Have you travelled to the Outback before?"

Derryl hadn't asked that question. "Uluru and the Olgas, Katajuta—but that was years ago. An unforgettable experience I want to renew."

"I'm sure we can arrange it," he said smoothly. "Now, I'd like you to come aboard." He shot a look over Genevieve's head to where his self-alleged badly-done-by brother was standing watching them—not with detachment, but with frowning interest. "Derryl, could you bring Genevieve's luggage? We need to get away as soon as possible."

Derryl's muffled reply held irritation, which his brother ignored. Obviously Derryl thought his position in the scheme of things put him far above hauling luggage.

It was hard to stop herself from being *thrilled*. She was going on a journey that might take her to the brink of discovery. Potentially dangerous or not, she was on her way. Plenty of women would fall down in unabashed adoration before Bret Trevelyan. She was not going to be one of them. Every moment, every minute, every day she had to keep in mind her kinswoman Catherine, who had lost her young life on Djangala Station. Had she made a fatal mistake falling in love with Geraint Trevelyan, a man beyond any doubt the wrong man for her? Falling in love with the wrong man could be dangerous. Historically, there were mountains of evidence of that.

Trevelyan would be dropping the cattlemen off along the way. He made brief introductions, and all four men responded with genuine friendliness and courtesy.

Less than five minutes later they were all seated in a superior styled and fitted-out cabin. She could see that the very comfortable fully articulated club seating had been configured for the cattlemen to continue their discussions in private. She sat farther back in the aircraft, pretty well on her own, which suited her, marvelling at the state-of-the-art technology—fingertip controls, an audio-visual system, LED lighting, etc. Aft was a restroom, no doubt offering toilet, vanity and other upmarket amenities.

They were underway. The aircraft was taxiing down the runway, then within moments, smooth as silk, it gained height, fast climbing into the dazzling blue air. There was no loud drone from the twin turbo props. Inside the aircraft it was remarkably quiet. She could even darken the window, if she so chose. Derryl had elected to take the trip in the cockpit with his brother, which told her he wasn't about to waste time on *her*. She was grateful for that.

Some change in the aircraft woke her. A change in altitude. She straightened up, amazed to find she had drifted off. Smoothing her hair, she stared out of the window. Trevelyan was bringing the King Air around in a slow tilting curve, making a descent onto what appeared to be a fairly large settlement in the middle of nowhere. A whole collection of buildings sprawled beneath her, and further off mobs of cattle browsed peacefully on a lushness she had not expected to see. But then this was Australia—a continent of searing drought and raging floods.

The great irony was that the arid red landscape

had turned into a wild paradise. The Three Great Rivers system of the Outback—Georgina, Diamantina, Cooper Creek—now mostly dry, had run with water in some places fifty miles wide. What lay beneath her was the nation's fabled Channel Country in the remote south-west. It was the country's leading producer of beef, the home of the cattle kings.

The Great Flood, as it was now called, had filled every channel, billabong, waterhole, and clay pan. The floodwaters had even reached the ephemeral Lake Eyre at the continent's centre, the lowest point. Lake Eyre filled rarely—maybe twice in a century. She had seen pictures published in all the newspapers of the thousands and thousands of birds, including the wonderful pelicans that had flown thousands of kilometres to breed there. How did the birds know? They had to fly continual reconnaissance missions. But this was Australia—a land of ten-year droughts and monstrous floods. Somehow the land and the people came back.

She found herself gritting her teeth as they prepared to land on the all weather airstrip. She had never been ecstatic about flying, even in the Airbus. This flight had been remarkably smooth, but she wasn't at home in light aircraft, however splendid. Landing was more dangerous than taking off. The four cattlemen were ready to disembark, all four remembering her name, doffing their akubras politely. Painted on the corrugated iron roof of the hangar below, she had seen the name of the station: Kuna Kura Downs.

Derryl Trevelyan followed the disembarking cattlemen, talking all the while, Trevelyan came last. He beckoned to her, brilliant dark eyes continuing to measure her, the sort of person she was.

"Opportunity to stretch your legs," he said, a smile deepening the sexy brackets at the sides of his mouth.

"Thank you." God, how a smile could challenge one's composure! "But the seating is anything but cramped."

"You enjoyed the flight?"

She nodded. "I have to admit it was so smooth I fell asleep."

"Flying conditions were excellent," he said. "Come along. You might like to meet our friends and closest neighbours to the north-east—the Rawleighs. We won't be staying more than ten minutes. I want to get home."

She did what she was told. Trevelyan commanded. People obeyed. She felt a touch jittery, as though he knew all about her but had still allowed her to come. Surely that couldn't be so? He couldn't know about Catherine and the family connection? A man like that would be too busy to check out a mere ghostwriter. Something he might think akin to a ventriloquist's dummy.

A tall, athletic young woman, with long dark hair worn in a thick plait down her back, detached herself from the small group, running towards Trevelyan, arms uplifted in greeting, her lightly tanned face wreathed in welcoming smiles.

All hail the conquering hero!

Genevieve guessed he was long used to it.

"Bret!" the young woman exclaimed in a kind of ecstasy, launching herself at him.

Genevieve waited with great interest for Trevelyan's response. He didn't draw her to him, as the young woman clearly hoped. He didn't go so far as to give her the salute with a kiss on both cheeks either, but he did dip his handsome head to brush her cheek. "How are you, Liane?"

Information started to drill through Genevieve's brain. Rawleigh? Hadn't he once been engaged to a Liane Rawleigh?

No time to ponder. There were introductions

to be made. Up close, Liane Rawleigh put her in mind of a sleek thoroughbred. She was exceptionally good-looking, with ice-blue eyes in stunning contrast to her dark hair. She appeared unable to extricate herself from Trevelyan—indeed she was clinging to him with possessive pride. The engagement might well be off, but it was obvious Liane hadn't fallen out of love with him. So who had ditched whom? How had it come about?

Liane continued to hang off his arm while he introduced Genevieve as the writer his great-aunt had hired to help her with her book. Liane regarded her with what Genevieve interpreted as an expression of guarded superiority. Genevieve wasn't an invited guest.

Ms Rawleigh had an educated, rather assertive voice. "Have you ever done anything like that before?" she questioned, as though Genevieve's chances of successfully ghosting a distinguished biography of the Trevelyan family were extremely slim. Her air of general disregard struck Genevieve as very off-putting. In a way it was much like Derryl Trevelyan's manner. Liane's tight smile to her was a far different variety from the one bestowed upon the cattle baron Trevelyan. She couldn't see why, but Genevieve thought there was something vaguely *malicious* about it. Maybe it was a trick of the heavy-lidded eyes.

Super-athletic in her sapphire T-shirt and skin-tight jeans, she had a high full bust over an enviably narrow waist and slim hips, and as Genevieve was appraising Trevelyan's ex-fiancée, Liane Rawleigh was giving *her* a comprehensive once over. Women were much harder to fool than men. Liane would have checked her eyes, skin, hair, her figure and either consider she had deliberately played down her looks or she had little style to speak of.

"I'm confident I can do the job," Genevieve responded pleasantly, without actually answering the question.

"Well, I wish you luck." Liane spoke like a woman who never ceased to be amazed. "Come over and meet Daddy. He wants a word with you, Bret, if you have a moment. I should warn you, I think it's about Kit."

Trevelyan responded with an elegant shift of a wide shoulder. He had beautiful, thick raven hair that curled up at the collar of his bush shirt. No time for the hairdresser, like his brother. He didn't have his younger brother's insufferable arrogance either—and he was the boss.

"Well, he is having a very tough time of it," Trevelyan commented.

Genevieve liked his compassion.

"Wallowing in it," Liane offered derisively.

Trevelyan didn't respond. He began to move off—a man blessed with vibrant energy.

Lew Rawleigh looked the part of a prominent, prosperous cattle man. The surprise was he was *short*. No more than five-nine in his high boots. Trevelyan towered over him. But his body was substantial—heavy shoulders, tightly muscled arms, trim through the middle—and he had iron-grey hair, charcoal-coloured eyes. He greeted Genevieve in cordial fashion. Certainly he was friendlier than his daughter.

"Ms Grenville."

"Please—Gena."

"Good to meet you, Gena. We hope to see more of you while you're here."

"I'd like that." A white lie. She knew Liane Rawleigh hadn't taken to her, nor she to Liane.

Genevieve had her hand pumped twice. She just managed not to wince. Trevelyan, a big man, hadn't subjected her to a bonecrusher, though she was sure Lew Rawleigh was unaware of his vice-like grip. His gaze was keen, as though he was trying to place her. That would be an ever-present anxiety. Some flicker of recognition. She was a woman harbouring a secret. Some might call it a guilty secret. She *did* bear a resemblance to her great-aunt Catherine. But her colouring was of a different palette. Anyway, Lew Rawleigh was somewhere in his mid-fifties. He would have been a small child at the time.

Nevertheless he would know of that early tragedy on Djangala Station. She supposed everyone in the Outback would have accepted it as a terrible accident. Sadly, people all too frequently stood too close to rocky ledges, shelves of cliffs, even precipices. The thrill was in the danger.

Liane had lifted her dark head eagerly to Trevelyan, all sweetness and light. "You're going to come up to the house for coffee, aren't you, Bret?" she urged. "Derryl said he'd like some."

Trevelyan declined. "I'm really sorry, Liane, but I need to get back. Another time, perhaps?"

The sweetness vanished. Liane couldn't control her reaction. "God, you spend too much time on Djangala as it is!" She couldn't hide her disappointment, or the edge of anger in her voice.

"That's my job, Liane," he said smoothly, but with an air of finality.

Clearly this was a very sore point with Liane. To Genevieve's keenly observant eyes Trevelyan looked utterly unmoved, although Genevieve could sense upset as well as sexual excitement in Liane.

"Is there something you wanted to say to me, Lew?" He turned back to Liane's father with an entirely different expression.

"If you wouldn't mind sparing me a few minutes?" Lew Rawleigh shoved his large hands into the pockets of his dusty jeans. "I just heard the stock squad have frozen Kit Wakefield's account. Just about everything has gone wrong for poor Kit."

"All the afflictions of Job," Trevelyan remarked, placing a hand on the older man's shoulder to lead him a short distance away to discuss the financial plight of the man Genevieve supposed was a fellow cattleman.

"Poor old Kit be damned!" Liane huffed and puffed. "He's only himself to blame. His wife drowned in a freak flash flood last year. She paid a lethal pride for a piece of utter stupidity, but she wasn't an Outback girl. Everyone rallied around Kit—we were all very supportive—but before long he was hitting the bottle big-time and making a lot of bad decisions. I'm not the least surprised he's in trouble, and expecting us to bail him out."

For a moment Genevieve was at a loss for words. She felt an urgent need for Liane to stop. A young woman had lost her life. God knew the terror that young woman must have felt with a wall of water coming at her, the depths of anguish her husband must feel now. Genevieve shuddered in horror. Where was the sympathy? The compassion?

"Surely a year is a very short time to mourn the death of a wife in such devastating circumstances?" she said. "Heartbreak is very difficult to overcome. Lives get derailed. It would take a long time to get back to even a semblance of normal life."

Liane's blue eyes snapped back from staring after Trevelyan's shot daggers at her. Obviously he was the only one worth paying attention to. Everything and everybody appeared to be only a background for Bret Trevelyan.

"Armchair psychologist, are we? He didn't love her," she stated, flicking aloft an impatient hand. "He married her on the rebound. A case of catch-as-catch-can," she added cruelly.

Genevieve stared back through her round glasses, thoroughly dismayed. What had Trevelyan seen in this woman? What had inspired his love, even if it had only been for the short term? Okay, she was physically very attractive. And he'd probably known her all her life. The Outback was vast, but there were very few people in it. Proclivity? Everyone would know everyone else?

And Liane's way with him was vastly different from her way with anyone she didn't consider important in the scheme of things.

"What was his wife's first name?" Was it because of Catherine she had instantly identified with the drowned young woman, as if they had once been friends? Was she already drawing a connecting line?

"Sondra. Silly name."

"I like it."

"*You* would." Liane gave an acerbic laugh.

"And so would countless numbers of people," Genevieve said, torn by an urge to rattle Liane Rawleigh's cage.

Here was a woman potentially dangerous. A snap judgement, but she was pretty sure her instincts were spot-on. Liane Rawleigh was a proud woman, a vengeful woman. A woman who barely beneath the surface was filled with discontent, possibly a total dissatisfaction with her life. And why not? She still loved Trevelyan. The break-up of any engagement was an emotionally wrenching turn of events. No one knew that better than she. She started to look for excuses. Maybe the abrasive manner was a cover-up? It wasn't easy dealing with a sense of failure, hurt and humiliation. But where was the compassion for Sondra Wakefield, let alone the grieving living Kit? Liane sounded as if she despised Sondra Wakefield. That telling *catch-as-catch-can*. What could have inspired that?

"Are you certain it was a marriage on the rebound?" she found herself asking, in perhaps too probing a voice.

"I should be." Liane's glare was hard and intense. "Who are you, anyway? Some sort of counsellor? As far as I know you've been employed by Hester to do the job of ghostwriting."

"I merely asked a question." Genevieve's reply was mild, though she felt exposed to this woman's dark side.

Liane lifted a haughty chin. "To answer your question, *I* turned Kit Wakefield down at least twice."

"Oh, I see." Genevieve spoke as though she'd been offered a more than adequate explanation. "I understood you were engaged to Bret Trevelyan at one time?"

What did she have to lose by asking a few pertinent questions—or impertinent questions for that matter? She needed to know a great deal more about everyone within the Trevelyan circle. Throw out a few challenges if she had to.

"Nothing to do with you." The startling blue eyes flared like the sun off ice.

"Forgive me. I didn't mean to upset you." Genevieve spoke with what she hoped was an appropriate note of apology.

Liane shrugged, a bitter smile running across her mouth. "What happened was that I got tired of waiting for Bret to set a date for our wedding. It's always Djangala. He's married to the place. I admit it's a huge responsibility. Too much has been put on his shoulders right from when he was a kid. But I wasn't going to take *second* place. Not *me*!"

She wasn't speaking the truth. No way had Liane Rawleigh decided to break off the engagement. She was still crazily in love with him. Liane was also sure Trevelyan wouldn't talk about it, allowing her to put whatever spin she liked on their split.

"So how long do you think you'll be here?" Liane's eyes returned to fixating on Trevelyan's tall, commanding figure. Obviously every moment of time with him was precious.

"I have six months at my disposal." Genevieve felt a stab of pity for her.

Liane's head snapped back. "Surely it won't take that long?" She looked as if she was struggling to come to terms with it. "Hester has gathered all possible documentation. You won't have to conduct any searches. She's been at it like a bower bird for years on end. She has the Trevelyan family history at her fingertips—both from Cornwall and Australia."

"Six months isn't a long time," Genevieve pointed out. "I'm surprised you would think it is. The first draft must be completed. The final draft can be done elsewhere, but I'll have my work cut out even then."

"Well, that's what you're here for, isn't it?" Liane asked with cold rationalisation. "To work?"

"Certainly. But I intend to take my time off. I want to see Uluru and the Olgas again. Bret did say he would make that possible."

The finely arched black brows shot to her hairline. "*Bret* did?" Liane's stare could have drilled a hole in a steel door. She actually looked quite savage. They might have been enemies on a battlefield.

"I imagine he could organise it," Genevieve responded with composure. "He didn't say *he* would take me, of course. I appreciate he's a very busy man. Maybe Derryl?"

A look of amusement crossed Liane's high-mettled face. "You're not Derryl's type, my dear. Derryl likes glamour girls, not academics. Besides, Derryl can't fly the Beechcraft. I wouldn't go making any plans either. Hester will keep you extremely busy. She's a very domineering old b—biddy." She'd nearly said *bitch*—stopped just in time. "Thinks she's far more important in the scheme of things than she is. We never did get on. I tried, but pretty soon I didn't bother. I know she did her utmost to influence Bret against me. Unforgivable in my book. Don't worry, Ms Grenville, you'll be expected to toe a fine line."

"I assure you I haven't thought differently." Genevieve's answer was mild. "Nevertheless, I'm entitled to my time off. That was part of our agreement."

"Make sure Uluru and the Olgas are your *only* distractions." Liane's stare was very direct.

It was an unequivocal warning.

"What are you saying?"

"You *know* what I'm saying," Liane answered bluntly. "You're not that dumb."

Genevieve gave a faint laugh. "I'm not dumb at all."

"No, just dull."

Genevieve didn't respond to the jibe. "So why are you worried?" She decided to have a crack at Liane. It wasn't as though she was in any danger of becoming Liane's next best friend.

"Worried?" Liane sounded furiously affronted.

Genevieve pressed on regardless. "You have no need to be. I promise I won't lose sight of why I'm here."

It was as well Trevelyan was coming back. She'd had about enough of Liane, who would have her work cut out, constantly warning off any young woman she perceived to be a threat.

Even a dull ghostwriter who just happened to be hiding in plain sight.

CHAPTER THREE

GENEVIEVE had never seen anything like the remote splendour of Djangala. The sun blazed down on innumerable lagoons, creeks, swamps, and billabongs, the water throwing back reflections of thousands of small suns and glittery pinpoints of diamond-like light. Anyone would have been thrilled by it all. She was conscious of nature and its power as she had never been in the city. Nature was sublime—whether it worked for you or catastrophically against you.

All the waterways were bordered by verdant trees and vegetation in striking contrast to the rust-red of the plains that stretched away to the horizons. Desert oaks dotted the vast empty terrain, and acacias more abundant than gums in arid areas, with large areas of mulga woodlands that abounded with what seemed like thousands and thousands of small yellow wildflowers.

A hundred or more emu—Australia's endemic flightless bird—disturbed by the descending aircraft, were streaking across the landscape at a rate of knots. She knew when threatened they could reach speeds of up to sixty miles per hour. It was fascinating to watch their flight. The kangaroos had to be taking their midday siesta. She could only spot ten or so, in a loosely knit group. Some were standing upright like a man, balancing on powerfully muscular hind legs and long tail, others were attending meticulously to their grooming, licking their forearms. It was an endearing sight to see the two wild animals that held the nation's coat of arms aloft in their natural habitat.

The great Djangala herd, like that of its neighbouring station, Kuna Kura Downs, was strung out across the open plains. Large sections were being driven towards waterholes to drink.

There couldn't have been a better way to appreciate the awe-inspiring landscape than from the air. From her wonderful vantage point she could look down on Djangala's homestead, surrounded at a distance by numerous satellite buildings. It was a far bigger enterprise than Kuna Kura. She was struck by the thought that, had things gone to plan, two Outback dynasties might have been united in marriage.

And aren't you glad it didn't happen?

Safely on the ground, they were met by a Jeep manned by a laconic individual called Jeff, who was waiting to drive them up to the house. The way he straightened immediately out of his slouch told Genevieve the boss was held in very high regard indeed. She supposed out here Trevelyan was king of all he surveyed. Yet for all his commanding manner and self-assurance she hadn't detected any arrogance. Derryl, who *hadn't* inherited the reins, was the arrogant one.

The long driveway was an *allee* of long-established palms with waving mop-heads. Genevieve sat forward as they approached the main compound, with its eight-foot-high enclosing wall that offered protection against the dust storms that periodically swept in from the desert. The towering sand hills had been an amazing sight from the air, running as they did in parallel lines, like the giant waves of the ocean. The sand even gave the illusion of being composed of silk.

An extremely vigorous climber with glossy heart-shaped leaves and great sprays of white tubular flowers fell in thick latticework over the wall. The creeper conveyed an astonishing air of exotic lushness in the semi-desert. As they neared the impressive gold-tipped black wrought-iron gate, flanked by huge date palms, it suddenly parted in the middle, and each half slowly pulled back to the side as Jeff operated the controls.

They were inside the Trevelyan desert fortress at last!

It was a fantasy land of its kind, Genevieve thought. So *isolated*. If one wanted to leave one couldn't simply jump in a car and drive off in a big hurry. By air was really the only way out. In the past, tourists not sufficiently respectful of the dangers of this desert heartland had come to grief—some dying, others mercifully saved by land or aerial surveillance.

Genevieve looked about her with intense concentration, storing up everything for the future. That was what made her a writer. She had studied various photographs of Djangala Station in large coffee table books featuring many of the country's finest properties. The photographs didn't do the homestead justice. Nor could the photographs convey how utterly bizarre it was to come upon such a mansion set in the middle of nowhere. But then she remembered the homestead had had as much importance to early settlers as the castle to an English lord. A homestead was any rural dwelling, but Djangala was the homestead of the "landed aristocracy"—the great pioneering families who, regardless of where they settled to make their fortunes, built houses of long-term permanence to proclaim their success.

Djangala wasn't the traditional kind of Georgian house "gentleman squatters" in Tasmania, New South Wales, and Victoria had built in memory of the Old Country, the place of their birth. Djangala homestead, a twenty-room mansion, had a decidedly Spanish look. How intriguing! Maybe Richard Trevelyan, who had built it, had taken the Grand Tour of Europe and retained an image of the sort of house he wanted to build? Whatever its architecture, the mansion, constructed of finely cut sandstone, had a wonderfully romantic appeal. A two-storey central section with an arched colonnade was flanked on either side by tall rectangular wings. The upper floor, probably bedrooms, was decorated with little curved balconies that overlooked the landscaped grounds. Four chimneys sat atop the terracotta-tiled roof. She knew from past trips to the Red Centre that desert sands cooled down amazingly at night.

This definitely was *not* a humble abode. Genevieve wondered if Catherine had found her first sight of Djangala homestead as thrilling as she did. Had Catherine felt the same buzz of excitement? Only what had started for Catherine as a welcome invitation to visit a historic station had ended in a terrifying experience and death. Life could be destroyed in a second. Accident or not? That was what she was here to determine. She could almost see Catherine out of the corner of her eye. Catherine of the long blonde hair and radiant blue eyes. Catherine, forever young.

Her thoughts sobered. Many things weren't as they seemed. No one really knew what had happened. Catherine had been alone at the time.

Or had she?

Had the policeman in charge of the investigation checked out alibis, or were the Trevelyans too highly esteemed to have to account for themselves?

Trevelyan, standing a little distance off, was struck by the demeanour of the young woman Hester had chosen to ghostwrite the family history. At the moment she appeared caught in a reverie he thought oddly melancholic, as though she was trying to silence some mournful voice in her head. Maybe she was struggling with personal hurt or disappointment? He supposed it would come out sooner or later.

It was he who had allowed this to happen, by giving Hester the go-ahead. It had been in the nature of giving her something to fill her time and her active mind, but he was fully prepared to self-publish—if the book was ever finished, that was. It had started out as a simple exercise in humouring Hester, but the downside was that he was becoming increasingly wary of having many of the old stories raked up. On a historic station like Djangala there were lots of stories to be told.

One he preferred not to be exposed again to the light of day was the tragic death of his grandmother's friend, Catherine Lytton. The verdict had been accidental death, but he had always had the uncomfortable feeling something wasn't quite right. He had no proof. He'd been born well over twenty years later, and as far as he could establish there had been no hint of foul play—just this unspoken gut feeling. He knew his father had experienced it too. Catherine Lytton, over the years, had grown to be a taboo subject.

There were other things he preferred not to get into print too. His father's accidental death at the hands of a visitor to the station unused to fire arms. The visitor had been devastated at the time, blaming himself terribly. Then there was the ugly break up of his parents' marriage, and his mother's defection with a family friend. Oddly, she had never married him after the divorce came through. The great rift had never been mended.

All in all there were many things he would prefer to remain private. God knew there was enough *safe* material.

Genevieve Grenville intrigued him. Instinct told him she was a woman in disguise: a young woman playing a role. The lenses in her bookish spectacles were clear glass—a dead giveaway. What was the reason behind that? Another thing: here was a beautiful woman going all out not to draw attention to herself. Again, why? Playing it safe? Was she in hiding for some reason? Or did she think she would make a better impression on Hester if she damped her looks way down? Perhaps that was it.

When he had the time he would check Ms Genevieve Grenville out—although she came with excellent references. Apparently she had taught for some years at a prestigious girls' school— Grange Hall. Even he had heard of it. It was quite possible it was then she had begun to camouflage her very real beauty. Girls' schools didn't encourage fashion plates. Too much distraction for the students—especially the teenagers she had taught.

He hadn't missed the glorious flame of her hair—full of body, however tightly she had tried to control it—or the fluid grace of movement, the radiant smile, the flawless skin and fine features. Her large almond eyes were an alluring sea-green. He imagined mermaids had eyes like that. Cool, iridescent green. He even had a mental picture of her sitting on a rock, combing out her long hair with a seashell fashioned into a comb. The image amused him. It would be interesting to get to know the woman beneath the disguise.

He asked Jeff to take Ms Grenville's luggage into the house. Derryl had rushed ahead. It hadn't dawned on Derryl that Ms Grenville was not as she seemed. He hadn't bothered to take a close look at her. Derryl had a line-up of pretty girl-friends—all of them with big plans to land Derryl Trevelyan. They might well get more or less, depending on their viewpoint, than they bargained for. Derryl's temperament up to date had manifested itself as selfish to the core. He had often considered whether the fact their mother had abandoned them had significantly affected his younger brother's mindset. No one seemed to be able to meet his needs—although *he* had a clear conscience on that one.

For most of their lives Derryl had see-sawed between looking up to him as his big brother and detesting him, or his position as the first-born son, and then later his authority. Worse, on a working cattle station, Derryl *hated* work of any kind. So much so that he would have to make some hard decisions soon. Derryl wasn't carrying his weight. He knew the men were fed up with his brother's lack of commitment. His trusted overseer Steve Cahill had told him on more than one occasion that he couldn't rely on Derryl to carry out an order, when all other station hands jumped to as expected.

From time to time Derryl talked about heading off to one of the capital cities, but he never did. It seemed very much as if he had no real ambition outside of making life as easy as he possibly could. He had a long-running conflict with authority anyway: endless complaints and a whole catalogue of resentments towards their father, endless sibling rivalry with him. It had proved very stressful for the household.

* * *

"Ms Grenville?"

His resonant voice was a clarion call to the present. Genevieve spun quickly, coming out of her reverie. "Please—call me Genevieve," she invited.

He gave her another of those half-smiles that to her consternation caused the sweetest pain to her heart. Apprehension set in. She wasn't a free agent. She had to remember why she was here. Unwise attraction could lead into dark labyrinths. Unwise attraction could even undermine one's life.

"I thought perhaps I was breaking in on a private moment," he said, dark eyes studying her in such a way that a wave of heat rushed from Genevieve's head to her toes.

It sparked off a moment of panic. He was far too perceptive. The white smile in his sun-bronzed face was madly attractive, in accord with his whole dynamic. He had a beautiful mouth—firm, very masculine, sculpted with definite edges. She felt understandable alarm at the stirring within her. Trevelyan had such a compelling aura that her memory of Mark faded away into nothingness. How was that possible? Her fiancé, a lover she'd been intimate with, all but obliterated? She might be in need of a powerful distraction, but not Trevelyan.

"Why aren't you wearing sunglasses?" he was asking. "You really need them." He was watching the effect of the sun on her flaming hair. It was flashing out all the bright coppers, the rosy reds, the threads of metallic gold.

Genevieve looked down, patting the mustard-coloured leather tote bag she had slung over her shoulder. She wondered if he'd noticed the designer label stitched onto the front. Probably had. "They're in here somewhere," she said.

"Find them."

"I know an order when I hear one."

"It is."

"Okay." This was a man well used to giving orders. She kept her head down as she removed her fake glasses and popped them into the capacious bag, rummaging for her sunglasses. Tiffany & Co. Again the expensive label would stand out—like the sparkling silver circles on the winged sides. Couldn't be helped. Anyway, there had been no suggestion she was struggling financially. She'd held down a well-paid teaching job.

"Let's go into the house," he said, gesturing with his arm to the curving flight of stone steps.

"You must be aware, as a redhead, you have to be doubly careful in the sun. I don't want our sun to bake you." Her skin didn't have the milky-white ultra-sensitive texture of many redheads, he had noted. It had the luscious stroke-me creamy quality of magnolia petals. Still, she would have to use plenty of protection.

"I'll be careful—promise." Genevieve's musical ear was becoming attuned to all the whistles and trills that filled the air around them, the rush of brilliantly coloured wings. Birds would naturally be attracted to all the nectar-rich plants—the grevilleas, the bottlebrushes and the banksias, to name a few. "I've brought plenty of sunblock."

"If you run out you can get some at the station store. We stock just about everything—clothing, boots, hats, etc. Do you ride?" He found himself hoping she did. She was moving beside him with effortless grace, tallish, very slender, without looking in the least unathletic.

"I need to get in a little practice, but, yes. I learned to ride as a child. I love horses." Enthusiasm suddenly entered her voice, causing a charming lilt. "My parents bought me my first pony when I was six—a gentle little Shetland. I have to say I pestered them. My mother thought I was too young. She wanted to wait a year or two. But I got my way. Apparently I had a natural ability, and I had a great teacher. She was patient and kind and an expert rider herself. She always won prizes for dressage. I still remember groups of us going out hacking with her." Genevieve paused as if in remembrance. "We lived on acreage in those days—good grazing for horses. I used to ride every day when I came home from school. I did all the feeding, watering and exercising, as I was supposed to. When I was ten my father bought me the most beautiful Arabian." She didn't say it had been to cheer her up. "I called her Soraya, after the beautiful divorced wife of an ex-Shah—remember?"

"I do. She couldn't give him children."

"Yes. My Soraya was inclined to be skittish. I was thrown a few times, but I never broke anything."

"So your parents were indulgent?" They must have been. Buying ponies and beautiful, elegant Arabs was a serious financial commitment. Although the acreage lifestyle would have helped.

"Very." She averted her head, as though studying the superb central fountain—a focal point for the landscaping. It was playing, which she found delightful—silver streams spilling down over two great bowls like a waterfall. It added greatly to the illusion of cool.

"And your father is what?" She had unmistakable class.

"He's a lawyer," she offered briefly.

He let it go. She was prepared to talk horses, but not prepared to talk about family. "And your mother? Please don't think I'm asking intrusive questions. I'd like to know a little more about you."

"Nothing much to know," she said, her expression settling back into a quiet reserve. "I've led an uneventful life."

"Now, why do I think that's not true?" he said in a decidedly challenging tone. "You haven't told me about your mother. She must be a very beautiful woman if you take after her."

Genevieve was stunned. She'd truly believed she had made herself unobtrusive. Her efforts appeared to have made no difference to Trevelyan.

"I do take after my mother, but I'd hardly call myself beautiful."

"Nonsense." With his height he loomed over her. "The beautiful know they're beautiful—just as powerful people know they're powerful. Beauty *is* power. It's commonly accepted a beautiful woman has power over a man."

"You occupy a powerful enough position yourself," she retorted, to get off the subject of herself. She had the feeling he was determined on getting to know more about her.

"It's a life crammed with hard work, Genevieve. And I don't lose track of the great responsibility to use power for *good*. But we were talking about your mother...?"

She felt exposed again. "My mother died in a car pile-up on the freeway in heavy rain."

"Ah! I'm sorry to hear that." He spoke with very real empathy. "How old were you?"

"Ten. I'll remember that shocking day until I die. For a long time my father and I were in denial. It didn't seem possible. The light of our lives— there one day, gone the next. I learned then that there are absolutely no certainties in life."

"I'm in total agreement on that. You and your father took it very hard?"

"It was a terrible time." She swallowed on a lump in her throat.

"I'm sorry." He fully understood her pain. Probably her father had remarried at some time—if only to give his child a caring stepmother. Some very nice woman she could turn to—especially at such a vulnerable age.

"Will I be meeting Ms Trevelyan today?" Genevieve asked as they moved under a collonaded central section that was decoratively tiled. She was so in the grip of Catherine and her story that Catherine's shadow might have been walking with them.

"We'll get you settled first," he said. "My great-aunt will probably send for you some time before dinner. She nearly always comes down for dinner. Even on her bad days—and she does get them. Extremely painful arthritis."

"So Derryl told me. She used to be an accomplished pianist?"

"She was," he confirmed. "She had no real ambition to become a concert artist, but she was very good indeed. Music is still an essential part of her life."

"Of course."

He gave her a brilliant sidelong glance. "You say that as if music is an essential part of *your* life?"

She knew he required an answer. Indeed, he was endeavouring to bring her into firm focus. "Music *is* life, isn't it? It conveys it all. I studied the piano." She actually held a number of diplo-

mas. No need to tell him that. For all she knew
Ms Trevelyan might deeply resent any attempt by
her to play the piano. As it was, Trevelyan was
regarding her closely with those mesmerising dark
eyes.

"So you *do* play?"

"Not as often as I'd like."

"But you're multi-talented?"

She knew she blushed. "I wouldn't say that."

"So modest?" He laughed gently, but it was apparent he wasn't satisfied with her answers.

"Maybe modesty comes easily to me?" She
dared to look up at him. It was a mistake. She
lowered her head again in self-defence.

His tone was distinctly mocking this time. "So
it would appear."

The impressive double front door, iron-bound
and studded, was open on both sides. Trevelyan
extended a hand, motioning her into a great hall
with a wonderful starburst granite and marble
floor.

She stood perfectly still, trying to take it all
in. "It's beautiful," she murmured at last, genuinely entranced. The huge area was flooded with
light that rayed through a floor-to-ceiling transom
window at the far end of the hall. A large table

sat on a magnificent Persian rug. She had to tilt her head to look up at the massive carved wood chandelier, suspended way up. On the table sat a splendid stone sculpture of a horse's head. And why not? Horses on a working station would be a man's best friend. A dramatic arrangement of bush materials—vines, dried grasses with their "flowers", tall spear-like reeds—had been set in a large ceremonial Japanese blossom jar. It was very sophisticated and enormously effective in that huge space. A gallery ran around the upper floor, supported by carved timber beams with delicate black wrought-iron balustrades. One could look down from the gallery into the central hall.

"I feel like a visitor to a grand residence on open day."

"Not everyone is as enthusiastic as you." He cast an amused glance her way. "Some prefer the traditional."

"Not *here*," she said. "The environment is so important. The house is perfect. I love the dried arrangement. It has soul. Not Ikebana—I think maybe Rikka?" She turned her green gaze on him. "I know your family hailed from Cornwall, but surely the design of the house has a decidedly Spanish feel?"

"The design *is* in the Spanish vernacular," he said, "which suits the hot climate. My forebear, Richard Trevelyan, travelled extensively in Europe in his youth. He fell in love with Spain and Spanish architecture. He actually employed a highly successful Californian architect to come up with this design. You probably know many Californian houses are built in the Spanish colonial style?"

She nodded agreement, still staring with some fascination around her. "I can't wait to see the rest of the house."

Her inner voice broke in with a timely warning. *Shouldn't you be more standoffish? Lighten up on the admiration?* Life had been a tragedy for Catherine, who had stood on this very spot, probably looking around her with much the same dazzled eyes.

Trevelyan gave her a searching look. "Earth to Genevieve…"

She came out of her reverie, giving him a slightly bemused look.

A smile tugged at his handsome mouth. "You were off again. One has to wonder where?"

"Maybe the house is speaking to me," she said.

"You're going to have to—" Trevelyan broke off as a small, serene-looking woman with jet-black hair streaked with silver came quickly towards them, with such elegance and dignity Genevieve wasn't sure if she was a guest or staff. She was wearing an olive-green shirt with matching loose trousers. The material was silk. It was hard to pinpoint her age. She could have been anywhere between forty-five and fifty-five. Japanese nationality. That might account for the superb dried arrangement. Genevieve wondered how many years the woman had been on the station. And *how* had she come to be here?

"I'm so sorry I missed you," the newcomer said, with a faint bow that involved her shoulders and neck, bestowing a welcoming smile on Genevieve. "I had a medical emergency in the kitchen. One of the girls cut a finger."

"Not badly, I hope?" Trevelyan, towering over her, lightly touched her shoulder.

"No, but it did bleed. There's always some tiny drama."

Trevelyan turned his handsome raven head towards Genevieve. "Genevieve, I'd like you to meet Mrs Cahill—our housekeeper. She keeps the homestead running like clockwork. Nori, this is Genevieve Grenville, who is here to help Miss Hester with her book."

Genevieve put out her hand. Mrs Cahill clasped it. "I am happy to meet you, Ms Grenville." The ivory-skinned, unlined face bore warmth and pleasure. The dark eyes glowed like lamps.

"Please call me Gena." Genevieve gave the older woman an answering smile.

"And I'm Nori." Djangala's housekeeper didn't stand on ceremony. "Steven, my husband, is Bret's foreman. Let me show you to your room. I'm sure you'll like it. Jeff has already taken your luggage up."

Trevelyan glanced down at Genevieve, standing at his shoulder. "I'll leave you in Nori's capable hands."

"You're going out again, Bret?" Nori Cahill asked as he half turned towards the front door.

"Things to do, Nori," he clipped out. "I'll see you at dinner, Genevieve."

He gave her a brief parting salute. Astonishing the knife-keen thrust of pleasure she felt.

The gallery was hung with oil paintings—all very valuable, Genevieve saw with her trained eye. Some fine chairs were set at intervals, and bronzes on stands. Both sides of her family were collectors of art and sculpture.

"We've given you a guestroom overlooking the front gardens," Nori said, with inherent sweetness and courtesy. "Much of the house has been redecorated in recent times. Bret wanted changes. He commissioned a famous designer to landscape the grounds. He wanted the place transformed."

"I'm very impressed." Genevieve spoke with genuine admiration. "The dry climate native garden is spectacular. I love the great beds of lavender that got thrown into the mix. Lavender is a great survivor. And all those tall showy grasses, agaves, desert plants, the marvellous sculptural rocks and the swept gravel."

"The landscaper has much experience in countries all over the world," Nori remarked.

She hadn't picked up any Australian accent, Genevieve noted. Nori's accent was Japanese-British.

"Bret wanted the best," Nori continued. "Mr Trevelyan—Bret's father—overlooked the grounds almost entirely. He didn't seem to realise everything had run down. He wasn't—" Nori was about to say something further, but caught herself up.

Genevieve suspected she'd been about to say it

had been Bret's *mother* who had looked after all aspects of the garden.

"I hope you'll be happy here." Nori opened up a solid looking timber door, standing back for Genevieve to enter.

For a long moment Genevieve paused on the threshold, images swimming in and out of her head. She was experiencing another one of those moments when she had to draw calming breath into her lungs. If only walls could talk! She had a certainty—God knew how—that Catherine had slept in this very room. To her highly imaginative mind it seemed as if Catherine was a *presence* who had joined her on her journey, guiding her.

"You have a concern?" Nori asked, an upward note of anxiety lifting her soft voice.

Genevieve shook her head. "Not at all. It's beautiful, Nori. I hadn't been expecting anything so grand. I'm not a guest, after all."

"You are to be treated as a guest," Nori said. "This room suits you."

"I know I'll be very comfortable and happy here," Genevieve said, her eyes on the carved four-poster. It was huge, made of honey-coloured timber. An antique brass-bound carved chest—perhaps once a wedding chest—stood at the foot of the bed, that was an inviting *chaise* near the French doors, a sofa piled with cushions, a large ottoman nearby, two bedside tables with elegant lamps, a carved writing desk with a similarly styled chair. "Anyone would love such a beautiful room."

Above the bed hung a large oil painting of sacred blue lotus lilies floating on a green lagoon. She moved across to the desk to admire a lovely arrangement of tall, slender Japanese iris in an antique bronze container that had dragon ears.

"I know who the floral artist is now," she said, smiling over her shoulder at Nori. "You must give me lessons. The arrangement in the central hall is wonderful, and this arrangement so enhances this room. I greatly admire Japanese subtlety. Rikka, isn't it?"

A faint glitter of tears shone in Nori's eyes. "My mother was a dedicated student of the art. I am still developing," she said modestly. "Upright flowers and leaves form the basis of these architectural arrangements. The Japanese iris is extremely important. So too is the lotus flower. When Buddha spoke of flowers he meant the lotus. There is an abundance of both in the homestead's rear water gardens, and of course the lagoons are nearly always filled with waterlilies of all colours. They thrive here."

"In Greek mythology Iris is the goddess of the rainbow," Genevieve said. "You're a very artistic person, Nori."

Nori only smiled. "This room used to be blue and cream," she said, rather wistfully. "Exquisite old Chinoiserie wallpaper. But Bret wanted all things changed. I'd always thought it very pretty, but he wanted something different and new. The colour scheme is perfect for you, Gena—celadon."

Genevieve put out a hand to stroke the beautiful silk coverlet that matched the curtains. It was the same lovely jade-green, but different textured fabric covered the *chaise*, the sofa and the ottoman. Sheen came from a variety of silvery cushions on the bed and sofa.

"The Chinese began making celadon ware as far back as 200 AD, didn't they?" She was certain this very elegant Japanese lady would know.

Nori dipped her head. "It is said they were after the luminous green of precious jade with their glazes."

"And they found it. How do you come to be way out here in the desert, Nori?" Genevieve smiled.

Nori clasped her hands together. "My mother

died when I was still a student, and I was very lonely and sad. My father, who was an important businessman, could spare little time for me. He had his son—my brother Katsumi, who has since succeeded him. My father sent me to relatives— first in New York, then in Sydney—as therapy for me. A complete change. I settled better in Australia, and studied at Sydney University. Despite everything I remained very unhappy, although my relatives were kind to me. It was Steven, wearing his beautiful smile, who came to my rescue like a warrior of old. My father was much opposed to our marrying, but we made our decision the moment our eyes met."

Nori's darkest brown eyes shone with love.

"Steven picked me up on a powerful wave and carried me away. He is an educated man. He holds an important job. Bret thinks highly of him. I, too, am very efficient. I have settled down wonderfully well in this place."

"How long have you been here, Nori?" Genevieve asked, intrigued by such an unusual love story.

"Twelve years now," Nori said, with a look of surprise that it had been that long. "Djangala needed an overseer. Steven secured the position despite many others vying for it. This is a vast and very important station. Not all that long after the break-up of Mr and Mrs Trevelyan's marriage their housekeeper of many years left. She had an important allegiance to Mrs Trevelyan. Two replacements also left. Miss Hester was displeased with them. Finally Steven suggested me. I have no difficulty running a large house, and I'm an excellent chef. Since Bret has become Master of Djangala I have a totally free hand."

Which couldn't always have been the case. It sounded as though Miss Hester might have been a mite overbearing. "I'm glad you're happy, Nori," Genevieve said. "You have children?" she asked with delicate interest. She thought Nori must be in her early fifties.

Tori beamed. "Our son, Peter. He is a scientist. This year he was honoured to receive an appointment to the Institute for Medical Research in Western Australia. He is part of a team under a woman professor of the very highest calibre."

"He sounds brilliant. You and your husband must be very proud."

"Peter has always wanted to be a medical scientist ever since we can remember. Now, shall I send someone up to unpack for you?" Nori asked.

"Goodness, no." Genevieve smiled. "I can manage that myself."

Nori moved to the door. "I'll send a tray up to you shortly. You must want to relax awhile. What would you like me to prepare?"

"Coffee and a sandwich will do me fine." Genevieve smiled again. "Thank you so much, Nori."

"A pleasure." Nori gave another one of her quick small and dignified bows. "Come downstairs whenever you're ready. Settle in first. I'll show you over the ground floor. The bedrooms are all on the first floor. Miss Hester's suite of rooms is at the far end of this wing. Bret has the other wing. Steven and I have a very comfortable bungalow in the grounds."

Without setting foot inside the Cahill bungalow Genevieve knew Nori would have turned it into an elegant, serene haven. Most of the girls she had taught English and French had studied Japanese with another teacher. It was a language that had come to the forefront of the curriculum in the late 1990s.

She was sorry that during her time at college she had missed out on the new wave of Oriental languages, although most of her older colleagues had admired and envied her bilingual abilities. She wouldn't have mastered fluent French with a Parisian accent without her beloved Michelle.

CHAPTER FOUR

WHEN Genevieve was requested—it was probably an order—to go to Hester Trevelyan's suite of rooms, she went quickly.

She had spent the afternoon being familiarised with the Trevelyan mansion, which far exceeded her already high expectations. No wonder Nori was happy here. She'd been the best possible guide. Hester Trevelyan might be something of a disappointment in the *sympatico* department.

She had just changed her clothes for dinner. Again, nothing to draw attention: a navy linen shift dress that left her arms bare. She couldn't have borne long sleeves in the heat anyway. The dress, however, *did* skim her figure a bit too closely. Oh, well—she had no intention of appearing in a tent. Her hair, just as she'd feared, was already breaking out of its tight restraint. Little copper tendrils were appearing around her hairline and at her nape. They glowed against her skin. In a day or two her hair would spring back into its natural deep waves and curls. Couldn't be helped.

She stepped forward a pace, staring into the mirror. Best put the glasses back on. She already had the certainty Trevelyan saw something phoney about them. It wouldn't surprise her in the least if he told her to take them off.

As she hurried down the gallery, she took heart from the fact Nori had been nothing like she had expected. Maybe Hester Trevelyan wouldn't be either.

She knocked on the heavy timber door to be greeted not by a quiet voice, befitting a septuagenarian, but one that was strong and forceful enough to resound through the heavy door. Anyone else might have had to shout, "Come in."

She was grateful she wasn't a young woman desperately in need of a job, like the governesses of old. She had to recall Liane's bitten-back description that would have emerged as *bitch*. Ah, well, Genevieve was here now, and she had no intention of turning back. She had to get to the heart of things without dying in the attempt. Hester Trevelyan would have known Catherine. They would have been of an age. Perhaps they had become friendly? Much depended on when

Hester had been away, studying piano at the Royal College of Music in London.

"Are you coming in or not?"

Once she was inside, the voice had an even more powerful resonance, giving the illusion that it was bouncing off the walls. And Genevieve had her first glimpse of a born tyrant.

"Certainly." With composure, Genevieve walked across the room without once letting her jaw drop. It was quite a challenge. The suite was crammed with sumptuous eighteenth-century European furnishings Genevieve just knew were horrendously valuable. It all looked wildly inappropriate: the bedroom of an old-style monarch or perhaps a madwoman. The most ornate curtains she had ever seen in her life had been down to the point where the room was almost dark, when there was still blazing sunlight outside.

The atmosphere had turned *cold*. What was this ability of hers? A gift or a curse? Whatever it was, it had been handed down through the generations.

An elderly woman sat in state, straight as a ramrod, in an extraordinary gilt wood chair that had to be the next best thing to a throne. Her painfully thin spotted arthritic hands were clawed over the arms. She didn't look well. She looked wasted. In fact a bag of bones. If seventy was the new sixty, Hester Trevelyan appeared closer to ninety. She wore full regalia—a heavily embroidered silk garment, black, imperial yellow, flashes of a gorgeous blue, radiant gold. The last Dowager Empress of China, Tzu His, had liked to cloak herself in "divine glory". This was a robe she might well have coveted. Stick-like legs were shoved into elaborately embroidered Chinese slippers. Snow-white hair, as abundant as Genevieve's own, was drawn tightly back, thick and heavy against her nape.

They had a hairstyle in common at least.

The only feature that was brilliantly alive was her eyes, black as polished onyx, and unfaded through time. They were "family" eyes in the sense that Bret Trevelyan's eyes were black as well. But whereas his eyes were beautiful, letting in life, his great-aunt's blocked it out. Certainly her unwinking gaze was fixed on Genevieve with no welcoming light at all. Rather a gathering awareness, a grim stare that was filled with the unthinkable.

Recognition?

The stare went on and on…Genevieve persisted in holding it. How she did so, she had no idea. She had absorbed the fact that this was one ruthless woman. Powerful emotions still burned in her. They showed in the banked fire in her eyes. Here was someone who in a blind rage might well have pushed another woman over a cliff. She knew her thinking wasn't rational, but she sensed she had stumbled on an important clue. If so, things were starting to fall into place.

Hester Trevelyan settled her weight more heavily on her crippled hands before she spoke again. "Who *are* you?"

The jarring words set vibration in motion, giving Genevieve the chills. She actually gasped, as if exposed to a cold draught running across the room. Her very real fear was being unmasked. Could it happen? Did Catherine stand so close to her? Could Hester Trevelyan actually *see* a shadowy image? Maybe she and Hester were both endowed with a gift?

"I'm Genevieve Grenville, Ms Trevelyan," she said, as though utterly perplexed by the question.

"Of course you are!" Ms Trevelyan drew back. "You have settled in?" she asked, as though she didn't care one way or the other.

God forbid she should say she wasn't happy with her accommodation. "Yes, thank you, Ms Trevelyan.

May I say how pleased I am to meet you? I'll be most comfortable in my beautiful room."

A cold, patronising smile touched the old woman's lips. "I dare say it exceeded all your expectations?"

"Everything has *exceeded* my expectations," Genevieve said quietly. "I'm thrilled to be here."

"Are you just?" Definitely a snort. "You're here to *work*, Ms Grenville."

She made it sound as if Genevieve might well be called on to scrub the odd floor or two. This was a woman who had outlived her time.

"I won't let you down, Ms Trevelyan," Genevieve said, sounding appropriately earnest. "But I would like to confirm at this point I have the weekend off to explore the station."

The parchment face was further ravaged by a scowl. "You should remember I don't have the best of health—as has been pointed out." It hadn't been. In her letter Ms Trevelyan had professed to be in good health. "If we can't work during the week, I expect you to be on hand at the weekend."

"I sincerely hope you remain in good health, Ms Trevelyan," Genevieve answered, like a courtier. Obviously that was her allotted role. "I'm most interested in our project."

"*My* project, don't you mean?" Hester Trevelyan was still staring at Genevieve. Or was it at a wraith Genevieve had called to mind?

The Dowager Empress of China had often been described in books as the wicked witch of the east. She had a counterpart in the west. "Of course it's your project, Ms Trevelyan." Wasn't it said the wise man profited by appearing a fool?

"Although we did agree that my name, Genevieve Grenville, will also appear on the cover."

Scowling fiercely, Hester Trevelyan folded her arms into the wide sleeves of her robe. "Yes, yes!" she agreed reluctantly. "You can hardly be called *accommodating.*"

"I'm so sorry. That's what I wish to be."

The apology worked. Hester appeared slightly mollified. "So you were a schoolteacher? How deadly dull was that?"

"May I sit down?" Genevieve had to ask. She hadn't been invited, but what the heck?

"It's what we do, isn't it? Sit down? Take that chair." Hester spoke sharply, indicating a classical chair that had to be one of the least valuable.

Genevieve didn't dare settle back. The chair wasn't very comfortable, in any case. She sat as upright as Ms Trevelyan, ramrod straight, ankles together. "On the contrary, I enjoyed teaching," she said. "I found it very stimulating. My classes were filled with highly intelligent teenage girls."

Hester Trevelyan gave a genuine shudder. "How ghastly! That's the last thing I could have done. I have absolutely nothing in common with the young. What are you going to do about that red hair?"

Was she about to suggest options? Hair dye, perhaps? "In what way, Ms Trevelyan?" Obviously red hair affronted her eye.

"Your colouring is all wrong for out here, "Hester Trevelyan declared, the black-eyed stare quite unnerving. "I don't want to see you so sunburned you have to pack it in."

"I'm well-organised, Ms Trevelyan," Genevieve assured her. "But thank you for your concern. I realise one can't be too careful. I have plenty of sunblock with me."

"You'll need it. At least you possess a good speaking voice. I attach much importance to voices. I can't abide our Australian twang. Oh, another thing—those glasses? You're shortsighted?"

"Only slightly," Genevieve fibbed.

"They don't fit very well," Hester said, sounding half angry and the other half suspicious of something about Genevieve and her appearance. "You may go now. I've already told Mrs Cahill I won't be coming down for dinner this evening. I expect you'll be eating in your room?"

Without thinking, Genevieve answered, "I'm expecting to eat with the family."

Appearances suggested she was violating a rule. "In my day governesses and the like ate either in their room or the kitchen." Ms Trevelyan said, waiting for Genevieve's response.

She had a mad impulse to say, *Your day is over*, and tack on a fervent *Thank God*. "Mr Trevelyan made it specifically clear I'm to eat with the family," she said, in an appropriately grateful voice.

Hester muttered something beneath her breath. "You know, you're a lot better-looking than you seem," she said, her wrinkled brows drawing together. "I haven't lost my powers of observation, young lady. We've had good looking young woman here in the past. One, I recall, was pretty enough to take your breath away." Abruptly her breath cut out. She made a choking sound, thumping one hand on the side of her throne-like chair.

Genevieve was reading Hester Trevelyan's mind. *Catherine*.

She could feel herself start to tremble. Many inexplicable things happened in life.

"Shall I fetch you a glass of water?" she asked with genuine concern. This was an elderly woman.

Ms Trevelyan didn't even bother to respond. "Go on. Go!" she said, waving an imperious back-hander. It was obvious to Genevieve she wanted to be alone with her thoughts. She knew intuitively her looks had something to do with it. Had her hair been blonde like Catherine's she would have had to put a semi-permanent rinse through it. "We start in the morning nine o'clock sharp," Ms Trevelyan called in stentorian tones. "We'll work in the library. You had better be as good as I've been told."

"I'll do my very best, Ms Trevelyan. Good evening."

She was almost at the door before Hester shot off a warning salvo. "I want results, Ms Grenville."

Genevieve half turned, levelling her own eyes with the old lady's. "You'll get them, Ms Trevelyan."

Oh yes, you'll get them.

She knew Hester Trevelyan had had Catherine in mind. Catherine the young woman Hester had never been able to forget. From the moment she had overheard her grandparents talking all those years ago, she too had been caught into Catherine's story without ever being able to let go. Some people refused to stir up troubling matters from the past; things that couldn't be changed. She wasn't one of them. There had been no resolution for Catherine. That was what had torn her Nan to pieces. Catherine couldn't speak for herself. Genevieve had come around to thinking it was her pre-destined job to set the record straight. The disturbing thing was Hester had given her the impression she had been ferociously jealous of the young woman "pretty enough to take your breath away".

The big question was why?

That's what you're here for, said the voice in her head. *To find out.*

She wasn't walking blind into this either. She truly believed she had help from the other side.

They ate in the informal dining room, under the glow of an extraordinary wrought-iron light fixture. The table was contemporary, of bleached and oiled oak, as were the chairs—eight in number, with four set back against the walls. The soft rust-red pattern in the creamy fabric that covered the seats was repeated in the border and central motif of a beautiful moss-green rug that was set beneath the table. The walls were papered in stripes of cream and green. Above the long console lovely framed prints of Australian birds were set in pairs, from close to the high ceiling to about a foot above the console where dishes would be laid.

French doors were wide open, allowing the cool night air to flood in. A broad area of luxuriant green foliage and slender palms formed a background for a white marble statue of a seated Buddha. Nori—it couldn't be anyone else—had placed a large black ceramic bowl of floating opulent cream waterlilies before the statue as an offering.

This informal dining room was where the family ate. The formal dining room was obviously for grander occasions, when the station was hosting a gala function or entertaining visiting guests.

The meal confirmed Genevieve's belief that Nori was an excellent chef. She didn't serve the table herself. The various dishes were brought in by one of Nori's staff—a deft young aboriginal girl, who moved like a natural dancer around the table. Genevieve was impressed.

The aboriginal people she knew had a cultural heritage spanning millennia. This land was their spiritual bedrock. They had no desire to be parted from a land their Dreamtime ancestors, Super Beings with enormous powers, had created. Genevieve knew "the Dreaming" did not refer to dreams in her sense of the word. It was more about the doings of those great Beings. She had read there were many sacred sites across Djangala—rock art galleries. She had a great interest in seeing them. If she was allowed to.

Derryl was making a surprising effort to be pleasant. Trevelyan remained himself: a dynamic presence. He excited her. That was becoming all too clear. Indeed, excitement was a deep thrum resonating inside her like a bow drawn slowly across a cello. She even regretted her decision to downplay her appearance. She wanted to look beautiful for him. How insane was that? But she saw in this man something she had hungered for. *Passion? A passionate relationship?* She could see now that hadn't been the case with Mark.

Only fatal attraction could be deadly. History could not be repeated. Liane Rawleigh was still madly in love with Trevelyan. She had already given a glimpse of her hard, cold jealousy of any young woman who came into his orbit. There were many such women, Genevieve realised. Had Hester been one?

Trevelyan's smile inspired in her all sorts of sensuous feelings. It was wonderful the way it illuminated his darkly tanned face. She had to wonder how this man—a total stranger up until today—could seem somehow familiar to her. She wondered how *she* was affecting *him*. There was something that had caught both of them off guard. Something that wasn't easy for him. Or her. Derryl's start of surprise when he'd first spotted her after she came downstairs hadn't been lost on her. It must be her figure that did it. Her bare arms and legs. She couldn't very well hide away in a loose shirt and trousers. Not in the evening anyway.

Both brothers wore open-neck shirts, but in the finest cotton. Both had rolled the long sleeves back. Their trousers were beautifully tailored. She wondered if they wore a tie when that very grand anachronism Great-Aunt Hester joined them for dinner.

The first course came and went amid light conversation that drifted over a range of non-controversial subjects. Trevelyan had a wealth of amusing stories of station life at his disposal. Derryl, as was his way, let his brother do the talking.

Genevieve looked down with pleasure at the beautifully presented entrée—tartare of trout—on a white porcelain plate.

"Flown in today," Trevelyan told her. "With other station supplies, of course. It's a regular thing."

"We get barramundi, Red Emperor, Gulf prawns from the Territory," Derryl tacked on. "Salmon and lobsters all the way from Tasmania. Pretty well everything. Not like the old days, thank God."

"What are you talking about?" Trevelyan turned to his brother with an arched brow. "We weren't around in the old days."

"True." Derryl started to fork in.

The trout was diced and mixed with a medley of ingredients. Genevieve tried to isolate each one, meaning to ask Nori for the recipe. Goat's cheese, certainly, egg yolk, black olive paste, various herbs—parsley, coriander, chives. Other things she wasn't sure of. The fresh lime juice and zest was easy. The combination had been mixed, set in fairly big oiled rings, then taken out to be served on the centre of pure white plates.

"So, how did you get on with Great-Aunt Hester?" Derryl asked, clearly wanting to put her on the spot.

Genevieve looked across at him. They sat opposite each other on either side of Trevelyan in his magnificent carver chair. "She seems to be an extraordinary woman," she answered diplomatically, thinking that good-looking as Derryl was, he was but a shadow of his brother. That couldn't have been easy for him growing up. It *still* wasn't as a man. She could well see how Derryl's resentments had arisen. It might even have damaged his personality.

"That's not telling me much," Derryl jeered. "Ducking the answer?"

"I only saw her for ten minutes at the outside," Genevieve demurred.

"I suppose she thought you were perfect, schoolmarm and all?" Derryl gave an unkind laugh.

A schoolmarm who could very easily turn into the Swan Princess. Trevelyan sat nursing his wine glass, thinking his own thoughts. He had an urge to sweep those dud glasses from Ms Grenville's nose and pocket them. She didn't need them. They were part of her disguise. Better to let her be. He wanted to find out her *real* motivation for coming here. He couldn't shake his gut reaction that Ms Grenville had an agenda of her own.

Was she information-gathering? An undercover journalist, perhaps? A would-be novelist looking for inspiration for a book of her own? Perhaps the ghostwriting was only a stepping stone? Djangala was a veritable Mecca for would-be mystery writers, he pondered. He hadn't missed the intelligence in her sea-green eyes or her sharp perceptions. Sooner or later he would pin her down. She might be trying to make herself look as ordinary as possible, but she was a beautiful woman without even trying. Even her composure told of innate self-assurance.

She had beautiful long-fingered hands—not overly delicate, but strong. He thought she probably played the piano a whole lot better than she claimed. The Steinway here had cost a great deal of money. It was badly in need of *real* playing. Hester, now that she was crippled, couldn't even bear to touch the keys. She had instructed Nori to have one of the girls regularly run up and down the keys with a duster, pressing down hard.

"So when do you start?" Trevelyan turned to her, his dark voice smooth as molasses.

It was the sort of male voice that struck a shivery chord deep within her. She actually felt a kind of swooning, like a young girl in the throes of an almighty crush. How ridiculous! It confused and angered her. Yet she couldn't deny the coursing of her blood through her body. Hormones—God! She even found herself studying his hands. They were darkly tanned, very elegant in shape. Hands were very important to her. She could almost feel the *thrill* of them moving over her body, exploring her quivering flesh.

Keep this up and you might as well start packing, her inner voice censured her.

Good advice. The sooner she regained control the better. Blind attraction was a heavy burden to shoulder. As it was, she had paused overlong before answering his question. "Nine o'clock *sharp* in the library," she said finally.

"She'll keep you at it," Derryl warned. "She's a tyrant."

"Both of us know Genevieve can handle it," Trevelyan intervened suavely, aware their mystery woman was getting under his skin. That couldn't happen. He couldn't afford to lose himself in an ill-advised relationship that was bound to end badly. If she was going to go prying into Trevelyan affairs—and he felt certain she had that in mind—it would be into the family's past. For some pressing reason of her own she appeared to want to unearth some family secret—dark all the better. He took consolation in the knowledge that Hester wouldn't impart a single one of them—even on her deathbed.

The second course was being brought in. Slices of succulent roast duck with a golden crumb coating over a tomato and herb mixture.

"Nori is gifted, isn't she?" Genevieve said, lightly spearing a slice of duck. "Flower-arranging, beautiful cooking and presentation."

"She's a cultured woman," Trevelyan offered. "We're very fortunate to have her. She's used to beautiful and valuable things. We've never had such well-trained home staff."

"How she fell in love with Steve, I'll never know." Derryl's lip curled with scorn. "She had to be insane. He's a stockman, for God's sake, and her dad was the big CEO of a Japanese electronics company. She could have had her choice of plenty of suitable Japanese suitors."

"I wonder." Genevieve laid down her fork. "*Her* choice or her father's choice?"

"Now, that's perceptive," said Trevelyan. "And, Derryl, would you please keep your voice down?

We don't want to offend Nori. She just could come in."

"Sorry, sorry…" Derryl said, like a kid about to throw a tantrum. "Spoken by a man who never makes a mistake or offers offence." He stabbed at the roast duck in lieu of his brother. "I bet you found her totally unexpected, Gena?"

"Her being Japanese, you mean?" She sipped her glass of white wine—a delicious Sauvignon Blanc from New Zealand's Marlborough district.

"Of course I do." He gave her a hard stare. "We get waves of Japanese tourists every year—they're mad for the Outback—"

"The vastness?" Genevieve suggested. "The infinite horizons, so different from their homeland islands?"

"Whereas we have a whole continent to ourselves—even if most of it *is* empty," Derryl lamented—a young man who hankered after the bright lights.

"Then there's the uniqueness of our wildlife," Trevelyan turned his brilliant dark glance back to Genevieve. Her mouth had such a beautiful natural curve. She always appeared to be on the verge of smiling even when she wasn't. "Tourists are fascinated by our Outback lizards."

"They would be." Genevieve took another sip of wine. It wasn't the wine that was making her feel so heady. "Our *dracoes*—the Dragon Lizards and the Frilled Lizards especially. The way they lift their extraordinary frill is spectacular. Who wouldn't love our miniature dragons?"

"I used to have a passion for dinosaurs when I was a kid," Derryl interrupted.

"And saber-toothed tigers, as I recall." Trevelyan gave him a glance filled with humour and affection.

Genevieve was getting a much clearer view of the brothers. She suspected, for all his resentments, Derryl looked to his brother in all matters.

"It sounds as though you've visited Japan, Genevieve?" It was a perfectly normal question, yet Trevelyan fancied he caught the glitter of unshed tears in her beautiful gem-like eyes.

She kept her head discreetly lowered. "My mother took me the first time, to see the cherry blossoms. It was and remains one of the most memorable experiences of my life—seeing such beauty with my mother. I remember all their delicate glory. Our favourite spot was the view from the Meguro River."

"The blooming on both sides?" Trevelyan nodded

"You know Tokyo as well?" At last she met those dark light-filled eyes that gave her such a buzz.

"Of course we do," Derryl said almost fiercely, as though putting her in her place. "Big brother here has even been to Antarctica. We're world travellers. We're not stuck in the middle of no-where *all* the time."

"*You* especially," Trevelyan commented, with the faintest edge.

"Ah, well, I'm not the boss, am I? I'm not Trevelyan."

"You wouldn't have wanted to take the job on, Derryl." Trevelyan made a point of turning his attention back to Genevieve. "Australia and Japan have an excellent bilateral relationship, Genevieve. The two countries have grown closer and closer. We're partners in the Asia-Pacific region. I'm not exactly sure how many, but there are a lot of sister-city relationships."

"So you've visited Japan many times?"

"Of course he has!" Derryl broke in rudely.

A warning frown crossed Trevelyan's strik-ing face. It appeared to have a sobering effect on Derryl. "Japanese businessmen and important guests have stayed here. We export Djangala beef to Japan. Our finest merino wool as well. Our grandfather started diversifying very early. He was a visionary."

"He must have been," she said with admiration. "I'm looking forward to learning all about him."

"Oh, you will!" Derryl crowed. "Hester adored him! She might have been in love with her own brother, if you ask me."

"A good thing we're *not* asking you, Derryl," Trevelyan said repressively.

"Well, let's face it! They had one hell of a bond. So old Hester says!"

"Not unusual between brother and sister," Genevieve offered, finding Derryl's assessment provocative. Not that he would *know*.

"Tell Gena we own two of the country's biggest sheep stations," Derryl prompted, taking heed of his brother's expression and wisely changing the subject. "We're involved in lamb production as well. Bret is Mr Midas—a finger in every pie. I've tried to talk him into selling Djangala. It's only a small spoke in the wheel."

Trevelyan looked as though his patience was

running out. "Don't talk rubbish, Derryl," he clipped out.

"Over your dead body, eh?" Derryl gave a bitter laugh.

"It *won't* happen, Derryl," Trevelyan said. "Djangala is our ancestral home. It won't go out of our hands. Anyway, you're a free agent. I've told you many times if you want to pursue some other life you can. I'll back you."

"At what?" Derryl cried, exactly as though he was throwing out a challenge. "I'm twenty-eight." He spoke as though time was running out. "How old are *you*, Genevieve?"

"Young enough to tell you." She smiled. "I'm twenty-seven."

Trevelyan liked her steady gaze. He liked watching the lights from the chandelier flash over her glorious hair. He wanted to see it long and loose. Spread out on a pillow? It wasn't going to happen. Tendrils were escaping to lie like coppery gold filaments against her temples, cheeks and her vulnerable nape.

"And you're not married?" Derryl was asking, raising supercilious brows.

"I'll change that when I'm ready, Derryl." She wasn't at all rattled by Derryl. It was Trevelyan who was having the wildly unsettling effect on her. Probably he turned all that sensuous excitement on and off like a switch. His ex-fiancée was still mad about him. So what had she done wrong?

"You must have a bloke, though?" Derryl persisted, bold eyes moving over her face and shoulders. "Or have you come to meet someone out here?" He transferred his malicious gaze from her to his dynamic brother. "They all fall in love with big brother here."

"Dash the thought away." Genevieve smiled. "Finding someone, Derryl, couldn't be further from my mind."

"So *you* say! I've never met a girl who doesn't want to get married. I don't understand why you don't do yourself up. You've got great legs. Great figure now you can see it. And you really ought to get contact lenses. Those glasses are awful. They're not even stylish."

"Derryl, could I plead with you to *stop*?" Trevelyan intervened with heavy patience. "I won't have Genevieve embarrassed."

Derryl burst out laughing. "But she's not embarrassed, is she? Gena here is a pretty cool customer."

It was an assessment Trevelyan had already made.

There was a choice of desserts: crêpes with a mandarin sauce that had the perfume of Grand Marnier, or a heavier ricotta cheesecake with mascarpone cream.

Genevieve and Trevelyan elected to have the crêpes. Derryl had both.

To Genevieve's eyes, Derryl looked and acted much younger than his age. Probably his development had been arrested by having such a brother as Trevelyan. Coming from such a wealthy family, Derryl was a young man who had never known what it was to be deprived. No, that wasn't strictly true. He had been deprived of his mother—a huge blow to any child. But he gave the impression that whatever he wanted in life he believed he was entitled to. Throughout dinner she had been conscious of the undercurrents. The intense anger in him—partly directed at himself, mostly at his brother. The ambivalence suited the classic sibling rivalry pattern. Love and admiration coupled with jealousy and resentment. She was reminded of her own relationship with Carrie-Anne.

It was over coffee that Derryl asked if he could invite a few friends for the following weekend.

Genevieve had the feeling he was doing it for her benefit—putting on a show, intimating that Trevelyan ruled with a hand of iron.

"Why would you ask?" Trevelyan responded, controlling his irritation.

"You do think my friends are airheads."

"You said it, Derryl, not me." He turned towards Genevieve. "You're most welcome to get some practice in on our piano, Genevieve. It's standing idle."

She had seen the magnificent nine foot concert grand.

"Oh, for God's sake—you don't expect Gena to pick up where Hester left off?"

Derryl cried in near horror. "If she'd played the blues or jazz, even popular music, it might have been different."

"You don't speak the universal language, then?" Genevieve asked.

He gave her a resentful look. "I love music. *My* kind of music."

"What about you, Bret?" She was so stimu-lated—over-stimulated, really—by his company and Derryl's stubbornness that she was forgetting her role.

Trevelyan wanted to encourage that. Who *was*

Genevieve Grenville behind the mask? He had the oddest feeling he *knew* her. Not possible. He would never have forgotten. Yet he felt he knew her far better than he had known Liane, who had been fool enough to betray him and think she could get away with it.

"Hester could have played all day and all night and that would have been fine with me," he said. "Our mother was an accomplished pianist too. The piano was hers. My father bought it for her."

"Our mother who *abandoned* us," Derryl burst out, his expression full of angst. "She upped sticks and took off. Went on her merry way with George Melville. Old George—the family friend."

If it was an unhappy marriage the woman would have suffered, Genevieve thought. Derryl couldn't let go of his anger. What about Trevelyan?

Trevelyan's expression drew taut. "For God's sake—stop, Derryl. She could never have gone against Dad."

"Did anyone?" Derryl asked bitterly. "You're getting more and more like him every day," he accused, with a return to aggression.

"Just as well for you I am *myself*," Trevelyan answered bluntly. "Dad would never have given you so much leeway. None of which answers my question. Would you like the use of the piano while you're here, Genevieve?"

"It's okay to answer." Derryl gave her a malicious grin. "You look the sort."

"What sort?"

Derryl shrugged. "Serious as in highbrow."

Her laugh rippled. "I'd greatly appreciate it." She returned her gaze to Trevelyan, trapped by the intensity of his regard. This man was knocking all the sense from her head. "I'm very much out of practice." It wasn't true. She hadn't let her music slide. She had regularly performed at Grange Hall's annual concert. "Should I ask if Ms Trevelyan would mind?"

"She'd mind if you were any good," Derryl assured her in a sarcastic voice.

"I can understand that, in a way. She wouldn't welcome reminders of how good she once was."

"There's that," Trevelyan agreed.

"Hester would near hate you if you could play her stuff well. She's like that," Derryl zoomed back.

"Then I'd better turn down your kind offer, Bret."

He gazed back at her with his sparkling black diamond eyes. "I won't hear of such a sacrifice.

In any case, the piano was my mother's—not Hester's. You needn't worry about Hester. I'll speak to her. You realise you've as good as admitted you do play well?"

"Honestly!" Derryl groaned. "I thought we'd all settled down. I remember Mum playing. She didn't thump like Hester."

"Hester would have been trained to concert standard," Genevieve pointed out. "It wouldn't have been thumping, it was *power*. But if my playing actually does upset you, Derryl…"

"What upsets me is the fact we lost our mother," he cried, in a voice wrought with emotion. "She wasn't Hester's favourite either. Believe me, Hester is a weird woman."

Trevelyan held up his hand. It was clear he meant business. "Genevieve doesn't need to hear this, Derryl."

"But she's taking a big interest, isn't she?" Derryl countered shrewdly.

Another something Trevelyan had noted. He was convinced Genevieve Grenville was a beautiful young woman who wanted to get close to his family. He also thought her intelligent enough to realise she was already under his surveillance.

All of us are locked into something, Trevelyan

thought. Derryl had suffered and was still suffering over their mother's abandonment. *He* had his deepest emotions well under control. What motivated this iridescent-eyed enchantress who thought she was in disguise?

CHAPTER FIVE

GENEVIEVE knew almost immediately she hadn't been employed as a ghostwriter. She was meant to be *the* writer.

Ms Trevelyan had reams of records, endless memorabilia, documents of all kinds—wedding certificates, birth certificates, death certificates—heaps of photographs, all sorts of reports on the Trevelyan family's life and their increasingly important position in the pastoral world. Just to sift through it was mind-boggling, yet a fascinating challenge. It looked very much as if the Trevelyans had never thrown out a thing. Ms Trevelyan was definitely a pack rat.

A keeper of the family secrets.

Far from sitting with Genevieve—something Genevieve had been rather dreading—supervising what amounted to endless sorting, the old lady had taken off, trumpeting warnings as she padded away on her little ballet-type slippers. "Make sure you keep busy."

Will do.

"Morning tea break ten-thirty. Lunch not a minute before one," she'd added sternly. "Mrs Cahill will bring you a tray. I've had a word with her. Plenty of places here you can sit."

She gestured around the very grand library, which was said to be one of the best in private hands in the country. Genevieve the writer, with the boundless curiosity of a scholar, felt like a kid let loose in a chocolate factory.

"I think I'll go out into the garden," she looked up to say, fascinated by the wealth of old photographs under her hand. "It has a wonderful Zen quality." There was a beautiful water feature right outside the French doors.

She had to wonder if it was possible Catherine had somehow found herself in one of these photographs. Or had all trace of her been removed? That was the big problem, though, wasn't it? A clear photograph of Catherine—especially if it was black and white—might show up a resemblance, point a finger at a face that looked similar?

"Zen?" Ms Trevelyan lifted disbelieving brows. She was wearing what presumably were her everyday clothes: an ankle-length royal blue silk dress with a wide pleated sash. Pearls dripped from her

lobes, an important-looking opera-length strand reaching almost to her tiny waist. She stood arrested, a vaguely perplexed frown on her haughty old face.

Hester Trevelyan was a force to be reckoned with. What must she have been like in her heyday? Genevieve wondered. Small wonder suitors had made the decision to steer clear of her. Or had it been the other way around? Was Hester single by choice?

"I think the native gardens here show a great appreciation of their natural heritage," Genevieve said. It was true, and it might mollify the old lady. "Your landscaper did a marvellous job—the placing of the great rocks, especially, and the raked gravel. That's what puts me in mind of a Zen Buddhist garden."

"Does it indeed?" Ms Trevelyan looked totally unimpressed with the Zen concept. The famous landscaper had obviously gone too far in the wrong direction. "Please get on with your work. I'm paying you an excellent salary. More, I suspect, than you're worth—but that McGuire woman insisted on it. So, for that matter, did Bret. He's a very generous man. That's his trouble. So good."

Her face was transformed by a look marginally short of idolatry. At least one of her great-nephews meant a great deal to her.

Poor old Derryl.

A good thing he had escaped to boarding school, then university, Genevieve thought. She wondered if Romayne came back often, bringing her husband. Trevelyan would be sure to welcome them with open arms. Derryl too, for that matter. Romayne was his sister after all. Apparently none of them had thought to draw up a petition to see Hester reallocated. A Sydney harbourside penthouse apartment might possibly have been far enough…

You've only *just arrived and already you're over-involved.*

Her heart ached with the certainty Catherine would have felt just as she did.

She couldn't credit it was already one p.m. when Nori came in with lunch.

"How's work progressing?" Nori asked, putting a tray down on a circular table covered with floor-length tapestry.

The tray was set with a silver coffee pot, matching sugar bowl, a jug for cream, a beautiful cup and saucer, and a small plate of sandwiches cut into neat fingers. There was a chocolate cupcake for good measure. Nori knew Genevieve only wanted a light lunch after a good breakfast.

Stretching her arms above her head, Genevieve stood up, easing back from the waist to take pressure off her spine. "There's so much here to cover. It's been quite daunting to just get through this much." She indicated the documents piled high. "I don't think a single thing has ever been thrown out. I hope I'm not making extra work for you, Nori? I could easily come to the kitchen to collect my tray."

Nori gave a three-cornered smile. "Ms Trevelyan gives the orders. We obey."

"Or off with your head?" Genevieve let slip. "She did tell me to stay in here, but I'm going to take the tray outside into the fresh air. I love all the water features."

"Bore water. We are over the Great Artesia Basin, as you would know. Shall I carry the tray out for you?"

"I'm okay with it." Genevieve smiled. "Thank you so much, Nori. I'm hungry."

Nori laughed. "Good!"

* * *

Trevelyan's out-of-the-blue appearance in the library truly startled her. She knew his workday often started in the pre-dawn and continued until dusk. She'd been sure she wouldn't see him again until dinner. But here he was. Like some big cat, he made as little noise as a black panther taking its prey completely by surprise. How he had entered the room so silently she didn't know. He was wearing traditional cowboy boots.

"Did I startle you?" he asked, in a gentle so-sexy voice.

Genevieve felt the all-too-familiar rush of blood to her head. If she had any sense at all she would get to work on controlling her reactions. "Big cats must move like you," she managed.

"No big cats in the Outback," he said. "Though there have been plenty of sightings over decades of what a lot of people believe are black panthers and pumas over rural Australia."

"I know." She was as intrigued by the sightings as the next person. "I've seen footage on TV. They weren't very big dogs or huge feral cats. To my eyes they looked and moved like black panthers. Perhaps the progeny of animals that escaped from circuses? Or brought into the country as pets by

American servicemen, then released when the call came to go back into battle?"

"Well, it's a theory." He gave her a smile.

She bit her lip. Pain could be very sobering. "But there *is* evidence."

He shrugged a wide shoulder. "I agree. Working away?" He took stock of the pile of documents on her desk.

She took the opportunity to straighten some papers, badly in need of a breather. Powerful sexual attraction was a kind of magic. Only was this white or black?

"Hard at it, actually." Her voice, to her great relief, sounded business-like. "This is going to be a huge job, but fascinating. I didn't think I would see you at this time of day."

Immediately after she'd said it she could have bitten her tongue. His God-given magnetism was just too powerful. She hadn't had time to erect effective barricades. Whatever else she had come prepared for, she hadn't bargained on Trevelyan.

He didn't appear to notice the rosy colour that had swept into her cheeks. "I need to scoop you up and take you across to the stables complex," he said. "I'll be away Friday through Monday. Derryl can entertain his friends in peace. I have outstations to check on. You can pick whatever horse you like, providing I satisfy myself you can handle it."

All at once it seemed like a miracle to be young and alive. "I wasn't thrown up into the saddle before I could walk, like you probably were, but I did tell you I was an experienced rider. You obviously didn't take it to heart."

"I'm taking your *safety* to heart," he retorted firmly. "Come along." Another command. "I don't have a lot of time."

She hesitated for a moment. "What about Ms Trevelyan?" she queried.

He turned back to her. A gleam had come into his near black eyes. "There seems to be a misunderstanding here, Genevieve. *I'm* the boss. Hester will understand."

"Well, that's plain enough." She spoke too jauntily, but as usual in his presence she was thrown off balance. It was entirely his fault.

At least she'd continued to dress the part. She was wearing a white cotton shirt tucked into sensible jeans. In another life she wouldn't have been caught dead in them.

The stables complex was huge, with a large courtyard to walk the horses. Two young aboriginal boys were in attendance. Trevelyan waved a hand to them. They appeared ready to do whatever he wanted. Trevelyan obviously commanded an awe-inspiring respect.

In the end she chose a thoroughbred gelding. It was a gleaming dark bay. At their approach it threw up its handsome head with a fine-boned skull, nostrils flaring wide with life. The gelding bent its head as Genevieve put out her upturned hand, hoping the horse would lick her palm. It did.

"I'll be very happy with this one," she said. "What's his name?"

"What if I said Lucifer?" Trevelyan offered very dryly. "This is a big and potentially dangerous beast in the wrong hands."

"It's clear he likes me," she said, petting the horse and patting its glossy neck.

"It would seem so. Horses, like children, know who their friends are. But no promises on that one. The last thing we want is a mishap."

"Trust me." Genevieve turned up her face to him. She was unaware her iridescent green eyes were sparkling behind the lenses of her fake glasses.

"If it were that easy..." he mocked, putting out a hand to whip the glasses from her nose.

Instinctively she put up a hand. "You can't do that. I mean—"

"What exactly *do* you mean?" he challenged. "Clearly you've sought to make yourself look what my great-aunt had in mind?" He dangled the spectacles in front of her.

"How do you know I don't need them?"

"A blind man wouldn't have been tricked."

"Derryl was."

He laughed, black eyes glittering. "Obviously Derryl will have to try harder."

"Okay." She surrendered. "I wanted to fit the bill. Nothing too dodgy about that. Ms Trevelyan requested a serious-minded young woman. End of story."

"More like the *start* of one," he contradicted flatly. "It's so nice to see you without them anyway. You have very beautiful eyes."

She felt the streak of hot blood through her veins. "Thank you. But I'd consider it a friendly gesture if you'd return my glasses."

"Why wear what you don't need?" He held her sea-green gaze. It rather stunned him, his image of her as a mermaid. The initial image remained strong. Mermaid, water nymph—cool, cool crystal-clear green eyes. And the long Titian hair was the stuff of a man's dreams. Any man would want to take up handfuls of it and bury his face in the silky coils. He showed nothing of this. Instead he deliberately shoved the offending glasses into the breast pocket of his bush shirt. "What else are you trying to sell us, Ms Grenville?"

She pushed away the quick rise of panic. "Does anyone *ever* answer a question like that?"

"Probably not *honestly*," he said. "I'd just like to know what's really behind this masquerade."

"You count wearing glasses a masquerade?" she parried, and raised delicately arched brows that were naturally dark like her eyelashes.

"You obviously do," he pointed out, in a silky-smooth voice that nevertheless gave her pause.

"Maybe I'm not allowed to tell anyone." It came out a mite frivolously.

"You'd do well to tell *me*." He gave her a long hard look.

She sobered. "You're completely wrong. Let's call the glasses a minor offence." She changed tack. "So, when do we begin? You said you had limited time? I should tell you I like a fast horse. I love a good gallop."

"I just bet you do," he said, a sardonic expression crossing his striking face. He had seen her scintillating vitality from the very beginning. "I can spot a risk-taker when I see one."

"Surely not *me*?"

"Yes, *you*—for certain." He gestured to one of the boys to saddle up the bay gelding. "I'd like you to wear a hard hat." He reached for one of a few that sat on hooks.

From delight to dismay. "You're joking."

"I never joke about possible danger," he returned, handing her the black hard hat. "Put it on." He turned away. "Benny, saddle up Sulaimann for me."

"Sure, boss."

Both young men hopped to.

"The name of your gelding is Zimraan, by the way. Both horses have Arab blood."

Genevieve, busy with the strap beneath her chin, looked her amazement. "Hang on a moment— you're going to ride with me?"

"How else will I know if you're telling the truth?"

She looked aghast. "I'm not stupid."

"No, you're not." Lightly he tapped the top of her hard hat. "Nevertheless, I'm going to check you out, Ms Grenville."

The way he said it set off a long pealing of alarm bells.

The horses were saddled up. Genevieve didn't wait for assistance. She swung up onto the saddle, quickly gathering up the reins. After a few settling moments for herself and her horse she began walking, trotting, moving to a fast canter around the courtyard. Zimraan was very receptive to her every direction. He had a lovely smooth action. So far, so good.

The moment Trevelyan cast a hard, assessing eye in her direction, she was provoked into showing off. She stood up in the stirrups like a winning jockey. She wasn't about to submit to Alpha Man. She thought he should know she was no novice. The danger was he acted as such a powerful stimulant on her that she was falling out of character. It wasn't the right time to show off. But she had such a great horse!

Zimraan was dancing, nervy, practically begging for a gallop. She mightn't have Trevelyan's superb skill with a horse, she reckoned. He looked wonderful mounted—tall and straight in the saddle, his cream akubra with its crocodile skin band set rather rakishly on his handsome head. He wasn't looking at her. He was controlling Sulaimann with a practised hand. The tall chestnut gelding was also mad keen for a gallop.

"Okay, we're off." He signalled to her.

She turned her horse swiftly to follow him, relishing the rising excitement.

It was *marvellous* to be alive.

Trevelyan stayed with her for quite a while. Then, deciding she was a class rider who knew what she was about, he let her have her head. She took off at a spanking gallop, wearing the abominable hard hat. She had to. He'd insisted.

With a spurt of pleasure he found himself lining Sulaimann up to give her the race of her life. She actually had the superior mount. Suleimann wasn't his usual ride. His chosen horse, Moonlight, as pure a white as Carrara marble, who carried him sure-footedly wherever he went on the station, was tethered to a shade tree back at the Eight Mile. Knowing what he had in mind, he had driven the Jeep back to the homestead to collect Ms Grenville, who was turning out to be quite a surprise packet. He suspected the surprise packet could turn into a real handful.

He had no difficulty closing the distance between them, but immediately he saw her heading for a ruined and crumbling old wall he just knew in his bones she was going to jump it. Anxiety surged over him. He knew Zimraan was not just a good ride, he was a good jumper. But who did she think she was? A steeplechase jockey? He was responsible for her, damn it! Why *wouldn't* she be a daredevil, with that red hair? he censured himself. But she didn't know the terrain. That was the thing. The plains country wasn't like the well-trodden tracks she was used to. He felt like giving her a good shake when he caught up with her.

As she and her mount gathered for the jump, he knew a fresh spurt of alarm—this time realising exactly what was about to happen. What would have appeared to Genevieve as a fallen log in front of the wall, half-hidden by dried twigs and grasses, suddenly shot up, morphing into a five-foot sand goanna, black with light spots—the perfect camouflage. It dashed away with comical speed. Those goannas had such speed they had been nicknamed "racehorse goannas".

Genevieve would not have had fair warning.

Neither would the gelding. The gelding's quarters were already bunched to clear the wall; Genevieve was bent low over the gelding's neck. Horse and rider were certain they could clear the wall perfectly—only at the last stride the gelding propped.

Spooked.

It was Genevieve who shot over the wall, disappearing on the other side.

The muscles of Trevelyan's jaw clenched. God help him, he was *furious* with himself. The unexpected was always possible. He had explained that to Genevieve before they rode out of the home compound. Zimraan was standing steady, unharmed but looking like a horse overwhelmingly ashamed. Thank God the two of them hadn't gone over the wall. Zimraan might have crashed onto her. It didn't bear thinking about.

He threw himself out of the saddle. She was lying on her side, her back to him. For a moment horror tore him up. He couldn't bear the thought she could be injured. He couldn't go beyond that…

"Genevieve!" He shouted her name so loudly he alerted every wild animal and every brilliantly coloured bird in the vicinity.

To his enormous relief she swung over onto her back, of all things *laughing*. Perversely, that put him in a fury. That was *laughter* dancing in her eyes. From being desperately worried she might have injured herself, he was now in an irrational rage, and stunned that he could be. When had he *ever* flown into a rage? He couldn't remember. If ever.

She was puffing with limited breath. "Pride comes before a fall!"

He dropped to his haunches beside her, his expression taut. "What the hell did you think you were doing?" he demanded to know. "Couldn't you have contented yourself with a gallop?"

She sat up, all laughter gone at his expression. "You're angry!"

"You bet your life I am!" he confirmed. "What if I'd had to pick up the pieces? The two of you could have gone over. Zimraan could have rolled on you."

She tried to defend herself, although knowing what she did she understood his reaction. A young woman had met with a tragic accident on this historic Djangala Station. None of them could escape the memory of that terrible event. It probably haunted the entire family.

"Why are you hitting on the worst possible scenario?" she asked quietly, the breath coming slowly back into her pained lungs. "I've taken plenty of spills in my time."

There was a pallor beneath his bronzed skin. "Princess Anne is a highly intelligent woman and she would have trusted my advice. Not acted recklessly."

"You're joking!" She undid the strap of her hard hat, shaking her head from side to side. Thankfully the pins in her coiled hair were still holding, although long silky coils were escaping everywhere.

"I can't be," he said curtly. "I'm not laughing."

She knew she was expected to apologise. "Look, I'm sorry if I caused you worry. I knew we could jump the wall safely. God knows, it's not much of a hurdle."

"It's high enough." He chopped her off. "And you didn't know what was on the other side."

"Mea culpa." She struck her breast. "It was just so fantastic—galloping off into the far horizon, not a building in sight, not a single obstruction, those gorgeous little emerald and gold budgies winging overhead, pointing an arrow for me to find the way. All would have been fine—only I wasn't counting on the Komodo dragon." She gave a wry laugh.

"A sand goanna." He set her straight, strangely calmed by her description.

"The goanna wasn't counting on me either. I saw it a split second too late. I thought it was a log—it was so heavily camouflaged."

"And they're all over the place—the plains, the dunes," he said shortly. "Our Perentie is second only to the Komodo dragon."

"Good thing they don't feed on humans," she said, relieved that air was coming back into her lungs.

"You're safe. Don't worry." He rose to his impressive height, extending a hand to help her up. "Are you okay?" he frowned. "Can you get up? Sit still for a moment longer if you have to."

She pulled a wry face. "I don't think I could have taken it had you been *kind*."

"Kind!" he exclaimed, clearly exasperated. "You're pale." He studied her intently. *Pale and beautiful. Like a flower.*

"So are you." She cursed her too-quick tongue!

He didn't answer, but drew her strongly to her feet, keeping a hold on her arms. "Genevieve, you simply can't go haring off like that again," he said, his dark eyes filled with silver glitter. "It's for your own safety."

"I realise that." Her tremulous voice was betraying her. They were so *close*, invading one another's personal space. She had never been so conscious of *man*—the sheer physicality of him, the natural dominance and—she had to face it—the superiority in so many ways. "I failed the first test. I'm sorry. But I promise from now on I'll keep a keen eye out for wildlife."

"It's necessary." He drew in a breath. "We need to head home."

"Yes, of course." She tried to inject normality into her voice. "Are we still talking?" They certainly weren't *moving*. They might have been glued to the spot.

I'm in control, Trevelyan castigated himself sternly. *For now.*

He barely knew this woman. He was not at all sure of her or her motivations. He couldn't think of a time his instincts had misled him. The confounding thing was—and it came like a revelation to him—he actually *wanted* this woman. He had wanted her at first sight. He wanted to make love to her, to feel her passionate response. He knew she had passion in her. Hadn't she pierced his armour without even trying? Liane even at the beginning, the best time of their relationship, hadn't even come close.

The conclusion: he had to keep a tight rein on himself or the devil take him. Chances were she was deliberately doing a job on him with those alluring sea-green eyes. It certainly felt like it. And it was much, much too quick. Much, much too soon.

He had to play it above and beyond safe.

He let go of her, feeling almost totally back in control.

Genevieve, thoroughly unnerved, was shifting her weight from one foot to the other, holding the hard hat in her hand. You didn't get to choose the man who aroused your deepest, most powerful emotions, she thought. It just happened. In this case disturbingly out of the blue. With Catherine so much on her mind, a statistic came to her. In most countries of the world two out of three crimes were crimes of passion, jealousy the motivating factor. She had clear evidence Liane Rawleigh was a vengeful woman.

Who was the woman who had hated Catherine?

"You're sure you're all right?" he questioned with a frown, not about to be lured into touching her.

Genevieve snapped back to reality. "I'm fine."

She didn't look at him. It was much safer that way. "Why haven't you told off Zimraan?" she asked. "The gelding was the one who propped. A horse recognises a good dressing-down as much as I do."

"The horse wasn't at fault," he said, acknowledging that his anger had been a result of fright.

It was a long time since he had thought of Catherine Lytton, but for reasons he couldn't understand she was now like a shadow, passing through his line of vision. There were no known photographs of her, but he had learned she was very beautiful. Like this woman, who had the power to slow his breath. He had intuited she hadn't come here solely to work. Work had been a key handed to her to gain entry. There was too much going on with and about her. She had come to unearth Djangala's secrets.

Could she possibly have some connection to Catherine Lytton? Catherine had died tragically not all that far from here. It wasn't unknown for the ledges of escarpments to suddenly crumble. One couldn't survive stepping off a cliff. Oddly, the fingers of his hands were tingling—as if exposed to extreme cold, not the desert's baking heat. So was the nape of his neck. It was like a moment outside time.

He pressed on, stopping Genevieve's progress with a firm hand on her shoulder, fanning out his fingers. Her shirt was at least a size too big for her, hiding her breasts. The fabric bunched beneath his hand. "Who *are* you?"

His voice cracked like a whip. Genevieve whirled in shock, lifting startled green eyes. "What an extraordinary question!"

"So why are you taking in gulps of air?" He held her gaze for the longest time. This man used to far horizons.

"Because you're frightening me." It was the absolute truth.

The air around them was so heated it all but caught fire. "Could that be because I want to know your game?" he asked, with a decided edge.

"You have no cause whatever to believe there *is* one." His tall shadow fell over her. She was starting to lose her temper. God knew he was deliberately provoking her.

"I'm someone who has faith in his gut feelings."

He spoke quietly, yet his tone rather scared her. This was Trevelyan. He could have her off the station in less than a day.

"They've never let me down."

"Really?" She was straying dangerously, but

she couldn't seem to help herself. Tension was in her body language. And his.

He was still holding her in his searing gaze. "It could help to establish one thing. You're here to ghostwrite Hester's book. Is that correct?"

"Of course it is!" She couldn't look away even as she wanted to. She felt violently pinned—yet he wasn't even touching her except with his eyes. She had never known a gaze so *intimate*. She felt naked. Exposed.

"So why don't I think that's the exact truth?"

"Surely it's truth enough?" she retorted. "I come with excellent references."

"I know that." He shrugged off the excellent references as of no account. "I've seen them. But please don't underestimate me, Ms Grenville."

She couldn't hold back a provocative laugh. "As if I'd dare."

"It's risky, but you would." There was no answering gleam of humour in his eyes. "There's something else going on, isn't there, Genevieve? A hidden agenda? You can't or won't tell me because it could demolish your cover."

It was hard to think straight with him looming over her. *Dominated* was how he made her feel. Very female. She would *hate* to have him as an enemy. "Gosh, anyone would think I was a spy," she said, with more than a hint of sarcasm.

"Given sufficient motivation you'd make a good one," he clipped out. "You really should have let me know you're an expert rider, as opposed to competent. That was quite a performance. I loved the winning jockey bit. And you know exactly how to roll in a fall. You know how to get up and get back in the saddle. You can gallop like the wind even when controlling a horse that's actually too big for you. We'll have to change that."

"Oh, no!" She didn't want that.

"Oh, yes. You come to us hiding behind very unbecoming and quite unnecessary glasses. The clothes you wear—purposefully selected—are downright dull. One could weep for that. And I have to say they're too big. Even your hair!" His hand shot out unexpectedly to catch one long thick shining strand that had escaped the schoolmarmish bun she effected. He held it over his hand, seeing how it flashed copper and rose-gold in the sunlight. "With a mane like that any other woman would have her crowning glory on show," he commented, giving the escaped lock a slight tug before twisting it back into the mass of her hair.

It seemed to her that her whole body rose to

his hand. "I'm delighted you approve of my hair, at least. On the other hand Ms Trevelyan doesn't much like carrot-tops. I might well have missed the job had I flaunted a fiery mane. Is that so hard to understand?"

He gave her that half-smile that lifted her heart. "The short answer is *yes*."

"I don't see why. I'm in no way preoccupied with my appearance." Which was true. "I'm modest."

Mockery flared across his stunning face. "So you claimed once before. We both know it's not true. You can't turn beauty into something bland, Genevieve, however much you try. You thought there was a *cleverness* to it, perhaps?"

She looked away towards the horses, standing so quietly, their ears pricked as though they were listening in to their conversation. Then she returned her gaze to his. "I admit I wanted to fit in with Ms Trevelyan's request for a sober young woman. I needed to be taken seriously—not to be perceived as someone looking for a husband."

"So who have you left behind?" he asked, with such suddenness it shocked her. "I can't help wondering."

They were moving onto even more dangerous

ground. "What would you say if I told you I have a broken engagement behind me? Like *you*."

Stop, stop. You're going way too far. Remember who he is.

Only she couldn't stop. Strong emotion was pressing her into crossing swords with him.

"You might be just the right person to speak to about how to cope with the fall-out."

A complex intimacy was binding them inexorably together. There was more than a touch of sexual hostility to it: two people powerfully attracted, both knowing such attraction came at a price.

"Want to talk about it?" he invited, his tone sardonic and faintly acid.

"No more than you do. Let's say the past is the past. It's a big gamble, handing over one's heart."

"Is that what you did?" He asked the question as if he really wanted to know.

She sighed, dropped her shoulders. "That question has begun to nag at me. Did I or did I not hand over my heart?"

From her reaction it was painfully clear to Trevelyan the answer was a resounding *no*.

"Is that what *you* did?" It emerged like a direct challenge, though instinct had warned her against it. She wanted to rattle him. Shake him up as he was disturbing her. It was truly a thrill, stepping close to the edge. And there was that other thing: the change of manner was undermining her role.

Proof of that came like a great crested wave. "Why don't we put paid to all those nagging questions?" he suggested, his brilliant eyes hooded.

Time slowed to a halt. Years might have passed as she stood there, like a woman who knew something momentous was about to happen.

It did. The wave rolled slowly and powerfully over her. Once it entered the bloodstream sexual desire drove out all rational thought. She knew a fleeting moment of alarm. Her hard hat rolled out of her nerveless hands onto the fiery sand.

When his kiss came there was no gentleness, no tenderness, not even a glimmer of it. Only hard evidence of a man's hunger. Was this ecstasy or despair? Somewhere in between? Genevieve was beyond such reflection. She was somewhere up in the stars. Yet this could be the start of yet another catastrophe. History repeated itself endlessly. Humanity couldn't seem to learn.

All the while Genevieve didn't utter a single word of protest. One of his strong hands encircled her nape, drawing her close into him. The other took hold of her around her waist. Her body had ceded control with frightening ease. She might as well have saluted him for his victory. She hadn't thrown herself at him. He had *taken* her.

When Trevelyan finally released her, her heart was thudding and her blood was roaring through her body. She felt pure jewelled sunlight on her face and in her head; she inhaled the clean male scent of him, felt the hard muscular contours of his body, his arousal. She had let herself go, swept away by the great crested wave. Now she felt tormented by wildly conflicting emotions, and beyond and above all that a sense of tremendous liberation. Gone for ever was all thought of Mark and his betrayal. Nothing in their shared experience had been anything remotely like this. She did, in fact, put a hand to her fast-beating heart—as though it might break out of her chest.

Neither of them spoke. They were both quiet, both knowing they had surrendered to an explosive passion. Time now to *think*.

He retained a light hold on her shoulder, sensing without words that she was so dizzy she thought she might fall.

He was the first one to speak, releasing a hard exhalation and looking out over her head. "We have to think of that as an answer of sorts, I guess. But surely there's a measure of comfort in knowing you can move on? What was your fiancé's name?"

"I'm darned if I can remember!" She managed a wry flash of humour. "What about you?"

He turned her face up for a moment. "I could almost wish I trusted you, Genevieve."

"You don't?"

"Still waters run deep. Your emotions run deep. For God's sake give up the disguise. I don't like it." He bent to retrieve her hard hat, passing it back to her. "Put it on."

"Yes, sir!" she answered with mockery. "Maybe it's a good thing you *don't* trust me. Though why you entertain notions I'm concealing something, I don't know."

He considered that for a moment. "Now, that, Ms Grenville is a deliberate lie. You *are* concealing something and sooner rather than later I'm going to find out. In the meantime we've got a bit of a problem."

"Which is?" She looked questioningly at him, though the urgent clamouring in her blood had scarcely abated. Every muscle in her body, every nerve-ending, was drawn taut.

"Chemistry," he offered simply. "From a single kiss anyone would think we were both starved of love. I feel we should look on it as an experiment, like we did at school. You need the right ingredients to achieve a reaction, but only if you have the—"

"Catalyst?" she supplied. "You're saying that kiss was a catalyst?"

"You put your finger right on it." He was back to mocking. "But don't worry, Genevieve, I'm a man with an armoured heart."

"Good to hear. That makes two of us," she responded with asperity. "I'm not contemplating let alone hoping for a repeat experiment."

"Very wise," he answered. "And now that we've settled that small matter, I have many things to do." He was all business. "Think you can find your way back to the home compound without resorting to a wild gallop?"

She put a hand over her palpitating heart. "You have my word," she promised coolly.

CHAPTER SIX

INCREDIBLY Genevieve was finding her way through the masses and masses of material Ms Trevelyan had provided. Hester crept up on her from time to time, silent as a ghost in her ballet shoes. No doubt such visitations were to check on progress or, better yet, catch her out. Sometimes Genevieve thought that was what Hester really came for. To catch her out. Maybe send her packing. Only she couldn't. Then again, Hester wouldn't consider she had to abide by such things as contracts. Hester wasn't what one could call a *comfortable* person. In her heyday she would have been capable of just about anything, Genevieve thought. Which was monstrous, really, if Hester were innocent of any wrongdoing.

But she wasn't.

Unspoken words hung on the air.

The dynamic Trevelyan, that god among men, had flown off to check on Djangala's outstations. Pleasure-loving Derryl had had his friends fly in for a long weekend. Ideal with his brother away. Genevieve had sighted but not been introduced to a good-looking young couple she'd learned from Nori were recently married; the leggy blonde—Derryl preferred blondes—was his *copine du jour.*

Early breakfast was therefore on her agenda. She had to be up and away before Derryl's guests sauntered in. She lunched at the outdoor seating area, with the white marble Buddha for company, and had dinner in her room, brought up and taken away by one of Nori's housegirls. She was getting to know their names. She liked to use names. It was friendly, and the girls had lovely, unusual aboriginal names.

Some of the original letters and records were damaged to the point they were illegible, but she had reams of material to go on. She was finding the history of the Trevelyans in their adopted country so fascinating it was hard to break away from her desk. But Catherine's story—her all-important reason for being on Djangala—continued to colour her every thought and mood.

She had believed Hester Trevelyan would be an endless source of additional information, but Hester was leaving her to it. Genevieve had checked and double-checked all the old photographs, thinking one of Catherine with her friend Patricia—perhaps copies of the ones her grandmother had had in her possession—might come to light if only she looked long and hard enough. It was Catherine who sustained her all through the many long hours she sat poring over material.

Much would have to be rejected, but she had put a lot of what she considered necessary for inclusion to one side. If the book was to be a success, the Trevelyan story would have to make an impact. It would have to resonate with readers who didn't want cold facts and figures. They wanted *personal* things, real-life stories, to admire, gasp and wonder at. The text would have to be embroidered with a lot of rich detail. Readers would want to know all about the famous personalities who had visited the historic station.

Maybe she could winkle out a passing mention of Catherine Lytton, who tragically had lost her life in a terrible accident on Djangala? Tragic as it was, that would titillate interest. Readers would want to hear about Trevelyan love stories, the happy and the not-so-happy marriages, the births and deaths, warts and all. Along with the best and clearest of the old photographs. They would want to become involved with and fascinated by

Trevelyans as pioneers of the great Outback. Anyone who had ever played an important role had to be mentioned. Nothing truly relevant should be glossed over.

The problem was Hester Trevelyan was the gate-keeper of the family secrets.

This book was for Hester's own ends. A lasting memorial?

Hester had known Catherine. Genevieve had learned Hester had been present on the station at the time of the accident. And Nori had many interesting things to offer. But Nori would know nothing about a tragedy so far back. Or would she? She could scarcely start throwing out hints. Nori, quite innocently, would speak of it to Trevelyan. But she certainly wouldn't be asking Hester.

It upset her that Hester's manner with the charming and dignified Nori was little short of bitterly sarcastic and rude. Genevieve knew *she* wouldn't have been able to tolerate the imperious nineteenth-century duchess act for long. Most of the time Hester barely deigned to acknowledge Nori, but Nori, so highly regarded by Trevelyan, and more or less inured to such behaviour, combated Hester's arrogance with a serenity quite marvellous to see.

There was so much drama about these people and their desert fortress. Inspiration had not simply stirred in her, it had gushed into full flow. She knew she could pack the most fascinating and salient aspects of Trevelyan lives between the covers of an interesting book. She already had an opening sentence. Opening sentences were important. They had to capture the reader's interest.

What drove a man to the opposite end of the earth to found his own dynasty?

She would start with Richard Trevelyan, naturally. He must have been quite a man to quit his native Cornwall and set sail for the oldest continent on earth, half a world away, vast, empty, and so very strange. And she would be learning a great deal about Trevelyan's grandfather, Geraint Trevelyan, the man who had allegedly told Catherine he loved her when he was more or less promised to another woman—Catherine's friend Patricia. The Trevelyans couldn't escape Catherine, however hard they tried. Sooner or later Genevieve would get to the bottom of that tragic tale.

Dig deep. Dig deep. You'll have to dig deep.

Three days had to pass before Trevelyan's return. Genevieve found herself so engrossed in the

Trevelyan story that she spent much of her weekend off working. Nori was most concerned.

"You don't have to work so hard, you know, Gena," she said, shaking her head. "All Saturday morning, and now today?"

"I'm enjoying myself so much it's not actually work, Nori," Genevieve explained. "But don't tell Ms Trevelyan that."

Nori laughed freely. "I can't remember a single occasion when I've *told* Ms Trevelyan anything."

"I accept that," Genevieve said. "But please don't worry about me. I'm having a ball. I'm a writer, after all." *That was a slip.* "The family history is fascinating. There's definitely a book in it. How are you getting along with Derryl and his friends?"

Nori hesitated a moment. "They're no trouble, really. All they want to do is enjoy themselves around the pool. Maybe I could wish they didn't drink quite so much, but it's not for me to say."

"Riding's not on their agenda?" Genevieve was planning on taking out the sweet-tempered mare Akela that afternoon—with mandatory hard hat, of course. He who had to be obeyed had given instructions. She knew the boys wouldn't saddle up any other horse but the mare for her. No matter.

She had no complaints. Akela was fleet enough of foot, and she did have her frisky moments. She would have given anything to ride Trevelyan's glorious white stallion, Caesar, but there was no chance of that. Caesar was a one-man horse.

Derryl's current girlfriend, Nori told her, was not happy around horses. "I overheard her say she finds them most dangerous."

"Which they can be," Genevieve said fairly. "It's a question of mutual respect."

"I'll be glad when Bret gets back," Nori confided, ready to return to her duties.

"Me too!"

Nori's delicate black brows shot up. "Meaning…?" There was a decided glint in her dark eyes.

"Just a remark!"

Nori made off with a little happy giggle.

Genevieve could have given herself a slap. She trusted Nori. She and Nori had grown comfortable in one another's company. But still she had to watch her tongue. Nori said she would be *glad* to have Bret back. That didn't go any way towards the truth for her. She had found herself *longing* for his return. Did that add up to falling in love? Many attractive men had come into her life before

Mark. None of them had made a dent. Love at first sight had never worked for her.

Until now.

She oscillated between elation and unwavering worry. She should be resisting this powerful attraction that had so drawn her in. Instead one part of her—the least in control—was actually wallowing in the magic of it all. She could *see* him when she shut her eyes. She could *feel* him—feel the touch of his mouth on hers, hard, punishing, but lushly passionate, feel his hands on her body, his arm enclosing her as she inhaled the clean spicy scent of his skin. She was even dreaming about him, waking with a start in the darkness astonished not only by her own vulnerability but her extravagant reactions. It was all so unlike her.

She had never thought in her life she would meet a man like Trevelyan. And more than half a century ago Catherine had never thought she would meet a man like Geraint Trevelyan. Had that meeting not taken place, Catherine would not have met her own destruction. Echoes from the past should be giving her pause. Infatuation—whatever—could bring heartache and even harmful consequences. Poor Catherine, so much in love was gone, gone, *gone*. Never more to take part in anything under the sun. There had been no magic powerful enough to keep her safe from harm.

She did her best to keep out of Derryl and co's way. Not that any of them came looking for *her*. No one put a friendly head inside the magnificent library. Obviously not readers. It didn't bother her in the least. So far as Derryl was concerned she was an employee, not a guest. That was the message she had to heed.

Derryl seemed to derive power and a kind of pleasure from lording it over people. Trevelyan, Master of Djangala, a man of high achievement, had no such mindset. He couldn't have been nicer to Nori. She, along with the entire domestic staff thought he was wonderful. Genevieve had already learned every man, woman and child on the station felt the same way.

Towards late afternoon she called a halt. She was doing well. She put down her pen, then rose from the desk, spending a moment or two doing her usual limbering exercise to avoid backache. A comfortable gallop—nothing all-out—seemed like a great idea. It would help her unwind and straighten out any kinks.

She still couldn't get used to the incredible freedom, the vast open spaces, the aromatic purity of the air, the extraordinary *light*! She was longing to explore more of the incredible landscape. What were those pulsing fire-like glimmerings amid the trees? And she especially wanted to explore the chains of glittering billabongs. Nori had told her they were heavily carpeted with exquisite water lilies.

There was a profound peace about this ancient land. And a palpable near mystic power one couldn't ignore. The aboriginal tribes had lived in this land for well over forty thousand years. No wonder they were so closely tied to it. She hoped she could get to see the rock drawings in the hill country. She'd have to wait on Trevelyan's okay.

Hell might break loose if she disobeyed a direct order.

A voice behind her startled her out of her reverie. It wasn't that loud, but it might as well have had the power of a lioness's roar.

"What do you think you're doing?" Hester Trevelyan asked in her most intimidating voice.

Someone really should have stopped her long ago, Genevieve thought. Hester would have been a tyrant in the making from the cot. She moved into the room, a stash of papers in her hand. She was superbly dressed as if for a big occasion: a high-waisted Empire-style silk dress in silver-grey printed with tiny black leaves. More important jewellery. She had learned Hester was never seen without her jewellery. She probably wore it to bed. Hester was a lady out of her time.

Taking a leaf out of Nori's book, Genevieve answered courteously. "I'm thinking of going for a ride, Ms Trevelyan."

"Too bad." Hester eyed Genevieve with disapproval. "I want you here. I have all this additional material with me."

"And I'll be interested to see it, Ms Trevelyan," Genevieve said. "But I've been hard at work most of the day. Yesterday too for that matter. It *is* the weekend."

Ms Trevelyan tapped an arthritic index finger against the sheaf of papers she was carrying. "I hope you're not going to claim these as extra hours?" she asked, as though readying for a lecture.

Genevieve assumed an innocent expression. "Me? No. It was my own choice, and I'm happy to report considerable headway. I think you'll be pleased."

Hester nodded without replying. "You're a good rider, are you?" she asked unexpectedly.

Genevieve came up with a modest smile. "I started riding lessons when I was a child. I love horses. I love riding."

"I was a wonderful rider myself, don't you know?" Hester offered abruptly. "There is such grief in growing old. Don't let anyone tell you there isn't. It's downhill all the way."

Genevieve's tender heart softened. "I'm sure you were a splendid horsewoman, Ms Trevelyan. Were you never concerned about taking a spill and perhaps hurting your hands?" she asked gently. "I've heard what a wonderful pianist you were."

Maybe it was the past tense that did it.

"Really? You've been discussing me?" Hester retorted in a brittle voice.

Any minute now and she'd be in a rage, Genevieve thought. Massive invasion of privacy. "Not at all, Ms Trevelyan. Bret mentioned it in conversation, and there are many photographs of you at the piano. Beautiful photographs."

That was true. In her youth Hester Trevelyan *had* been beautiful—in a severe kind of way. Rather androgynous, now she thought about it. Hester in riding clothes could just as well have been a striking young man as a striking young woman.

A sound of despair entered that autocratic voice. "I squandered my gift," she said, like a lament.

For some reason Genevieve felt moved to tears. "I'm so sorry." She dared not press further. But it was becoming clear to her that Hester Trevelyan had suffered in her own way.

"Do *you* play?" Hester barked, as though these days music damaged her ears. There were strange glints in her sunken coal black eyes.

Sometimes only the truth would do. "I studied the piano for years—which isn't to say I'm good."

Hester groaned. "I hope you're not planning on playing the Steinway downstairs? Some talentless idiot attacked it last night. One of Derryl's featherweight friends. I was too exhausted to come downstairs and order them to stop immediately." Hester scowled darkly.

Genevieve too had heard the piano. Pop tunes, the inevitable *Chopsticks*, accompanied by loud hoots of laughter. The house was so big the piano hadn't been loud by any means. Besides, the lid had remained down, largely muffling sound.

"I would only get in a little practice with your permission, Ms Trevelyan." She thought better of saying her nephew had already given her permission.

"Tausig?" Hester fired the question, at once sharp and sly.

"Not until it hurts." Genevieve smiled. "A few warm-ups." Carl Tausig, the Polish virtuoso who had died at the very early age of thirty, had written books of finger exercises that could and did work miracles on technique. Every serious piano student had their book of Tausig. Plainly Hester had been sounding her out.

"He was Liszt's favourite pupil, you know," Hester said, approval, of all things, settling on her face. "Critics consider he may have been a greater virtuoso than the maestro himself. Anton Rubenstein thought him infallible as a pianist—never a single digital error. Fancy that! I have heard all the great ones. They make errors. Myself included—though of course I was *not* great. Just good. World of difference there! But I do have recordings of myself, you know," Hester said, with a mixture of pride and pain. "All the Chopin *études*, preludes… some of his most beautiful *ballades*. Beethoven's major sonatas. Brahms, Liszt…the others." She waved her hand like a baton.

"I'd feel honoured to hear them," Genevieve

said, thinking it a tragedy that Hester had been so badly crippled with arthritis. The degenerative disease had stolen an important part of her life.

Hester could not fail to hear her sincerity. "I don't know if I could bear it." She drew a shuddering breath. "Come here, girl. I want to look at you."

Instantly Genevieve's heart quaked. She felt the flush of panic. Nonetheless she did as she was told, moving closer.

"You're not wearing your glasses?" Hester squinted at her ferociously.

Genevieve could hardly say her great-nephew had confiscated them. "I don't wear them all the time," she said. Hester wasn't wearing hers either. Was that a lucky break or what?

"When did you first start wearing your hair in a bun?" Hester didn't mince words. "That *is* the natural colour? Not a rinse? You're not really a blonde?"

"Goodness me, no!" Genevieve managed a mystified shrug. "As for the bun—that happened when I first started teaching, I suppose," she fibbed. The fibs were starting to really pile up. That was worrying.

"You're a secretive young woman, aren't you?" Hester accused, looking through and beyond her.

"Why would you say that?" Genevieve was becoming increasingly nervous under Hester's intense scrutiny.

"Takes one to know one," Hester said, her smile not without humour. "You're a *ghost*writer. The odd thing is you do put me in mind of a ghost. Someone I knew when I was young."

An overwhelming sadness broke over her voice like a wave. Sadness? Genevieve was suddenly ashamed of all the negative thoughts she'd had about Hester. A vulnerable softness had come into the arrogant old face.

For a long moment Genevieve could think of nothing to say. "You cared for her?" she dared to ask eventually, as the opportunity had presented itself

"I *loved* her." It was an agonised admission. "Loved her," she repeated in a near whisper, her vision clearly directed inwards.

Whatever revelation Genevieve had been expecting, it had never been *this*. She watched in stunned amazement as Hester put a knotted hand to her throat. "She's dead, you know. Long dead."

Genevieve couldn't utter a word. What was

Hester telling her? She was convinced that in advancing age Hester was desperate to get some intolerable burden off her chest. She *had* to be talking about Catherine. She just *knew* it. She never discounted those strange feelings.

"I'm so sorry." She was perturbed by Hester's abrupt cave-in. "But she lives on in your memory?"

Ah, the fatal question! Hester didn't answer. Hester was in full retreat. As violently as her frail body permitted, she pitched the sheaf of papers onto Genevieve's desk, causing many to fly about like a fleet of paper planes.

"Go for your ride," she barked, returning to her habitual arrogance. "This can wait for tomorrow." She pattered away on her soft embroidered slippers, quoting Macbeth as she went.

"'Tomorrow, and tomorrow, and tomorrow, creeps in this petty pace from day to day to the last syllable of recorded time.' Make that the crack of doom!" she called back. "Sometimes it takes an awfully long time to die."

To Genevieve's sensitive ears, her voice betrayed the pain that was in her.

"Others die just like that! You know what they say, young lady? Only the good die young."

Genevieve could have agreed with her.

Catherine had been several years younger than she was now when she'd stepped off a cliff and into the great void.

It was no use. The night dragged on. Genevieve turned this way and that, plumped up the pillows, tried to nestle her aching head into the soft mounds. Only it was no use. She couldn't sleep. Her mind was too active. That was no surprise. She was like this when she was working. But it was Hester's extraordinary admission that kept playing over and over in her head, like a CD she couldn't turn off. That on its own was making it impossible for her to close her eyes. She had tried a touch of lavender oil on her temples and the nape of her neck. She loved the smell of lavender. But this time the old remedy didn't work.

She didn't know what to believe now. She was unexpectedly warming to Hester—*wanting* to believe she had nothing to do with Catherine's accident. Hester was Trevelyan's great-aunt, after all, but she was convinced that not only Hester but the shadow of Catherine was trying to tell her something. How did one communicate with a shadow anyway? It was the other way around. The shadow communicated with you.

She couldn't think about it any more. She had to break the cycle—otherwise she'd be a wreck in the morning and Hester might well be in the mood to work. She didn't normally resort to painkillers for sleeplessness, but she felt desperately in need of a couple of aspirin without delay.

A glance at her bedside clock told her it was just after midnight. She knew the first-aid room downstairs was well-stocked with everything that might be needed on a working station. Derryl's friends had gone home, and Derryl, no doubt exhausted from exploring his girlfriend's charms and other non-stop entertaining would be in bed. Trevelyan wasn't expected until the morning. She was familiar now with the layout of the house.

Once the decision to go downstairs was taken, she didn't hesitate. She slipped out of bed, reached for her apricot silk-satin robe, shouldered into it. She was addicted to beautiful lingerie and night-wear—the lovely allure of it, the luxurious feel against her skin. The matching set—robe and gown—had been expensive. But no one was around to catch her out of character.

A few downstairs lights were on. That came

as no surprise. Low-wattage bracket lamps were left burning along the corridors at night. It was a very big house. Some lighting would be necessary for anyone who needed to get up and go downstairs. The great house was hushed all around her. She really loved the homestead. It had enormous appeal for her.

She intended to shake out a couple of tablets and then take them back to her room. She hoped they would work. She hadn't settled into a quiet existence on Djangala. She had been propelled into a fantastic new world that fascinated as much as terrified her.

Trevelyan was in his father's study, rather wearily turning over papers in seeking a document he urgently needed to check: all to do with aboriginal land claims. He had flown in less than an hour before, his routine inspections over to his satisfaction, and he needed to get an early start in the morning, when the road trains would arrive to transport several hundred head of cattle to market.

He didn't smoke. He never had. It was the age of enlightenment. Why damage an all-important lung? He did, however, like a drink. Not that he would call himself a heavy drinker. He picked up the half-empty tumbler of single malt Scotch and drained it, tipping back his head.

As he righted his head a lovely flash caught his eyes: a female figure, moving silently, more like *floating*, towards the rear of the house. It might have been a figment of his imagination he was so tired. Only this was no phantom. It was a beautiful, breathing woman.

Ms Genevieve Grenville, no less. His tantalising, intoxicating mystery woman.

What in the world was she doing? What was she looking for at this time of night? He could have called out to her, but he really wanted to see what she was up to, this mermaid who had put him under her spell. He got up from the desk, moving with his usual light tread. A rush of adrenalin had rid him of any sense of weariness. He was on the track of the not so innocent Ms Grenville.

Right behind her, he was loath to put his hand on her shoulder and badly startle her, but there was nothing else for it. This was *his* house. Why was she roaming around in it after midnight? It wouldn't surprise him in the least to discover she really was a witch, moving about at will when all was quiet.

"Ms Grenville." Voice and hand swooped low and soft.

But it was enough to cause her to whirl, her sea-green darkly lashed eyes huge, almost on the frantic side. His physical energy seemed to radiate from him into her. "For God's sake, you frightened me!" she gasped, one hand going to her quaking heart.

"Good to see you too." His glimmering eyes began an exquisitely slow dance over her. He lingered over her long flowing Titian hair, her overwrought expression, and what she was wearing, the shape of her beautiful body touched on lightly by her robe, the curves of her high breasts. The rose-dark nipples he saw were peaked against the lustrous satin.

My God!

He had never seen a more seductive sight in his life.

"You're not supposed to be home until tomorrow."

"I'm *so* sorry," he said, feigning an apologetic tone. "Are you actually accusing me of upsetting your plans? If so, remind me to e-mail you next time. But I'm so *happy* to catch you out of disguise, Ms Grenville. What a metamorphosis!

You've no idea!" Now his deep, darkly shaded voice was laced with sarcasm. "I just *love* the nightgown! It's exquisite. And that wild, glorious mane! One could weep for the way you've kept it confined. I've never thought you anything else but beautiful, but now—I have to tell you—you leave me a grown man gasping for breath."

His handsome face bore the stamp of self-mockery. "I don't for a moment believe you," she responded severely.

"True. Absolutely true."

There was a provocative gleam in his dark eyes. It caused her to wrap her arms protectively around herself, all too aware of her *deshabille*. Her robe lacked a sash when right now she needed one. "I wasn't to know you were home, let alone prowling around," she said, sounding aggrieved. Why not? He stood before her—all six-three of him—the physical embodiment of splendid all-conquering male.

"Should that matter?" he asked in some amuse-ment. "This *is* my house, and *you're* the one doing the prowling."

He was enjoying taunting her. Yet it put such a sparkle, a rush in the air. Didn't he know *he* was the one with the allure? She found it as thrilling as it was intimidating.

"Excuse me," she said defensively. "I count myself unlucky to run into anyone. It *is* after midnight."

"The witching hour, don't they call it?" The sexy brackets at the sides of his mouth deepened. "Magic things are said to happen. Beautiful flame-haired witches roam around at such times."

She could feel heat high up on her cheekbones. "I assure you I wasn't looking for anyone to practise on. Anyway, isn't the witching hour three a.m.?"

"Why ask *me*, Genevieve?" His dark eyes sparkled. "You're the one with the powers. I am but mere man. Are you trying to tell me you wouldn't have dreamed of coming downstairs looking a veritable vision of man's delight if you'd known I would see you?"

"I wouldn't have ventured outside my door in my nightwear if I'd thought you would see me," she said sharply. "Now, is there anything else you want to say?"

He spread his shapely hands. "Now you ask. What the hell are you up to, for a start?"

That shook her—as it was meant to. "Why do I have to be up to anything?" she countered.

"Because you *are* up to something, Genevieve. I thought we'd agreed on that?"

"Not to my knowledge," she retorted. "You have a very suspicious mind."

"Of course I do." He gave her the benefit of a half-smile. "But who would blame me? Can't you see it's the secrecy—all the other stuff? The hairdo, the dreary clothes, etc—that's set me off."

"Dreary clothes? Spoken like a snob. A *rich* snob."

"That's nonsense and you know it." His tone was clipped.

"Okay, Derryl is the snob. You're the egalitarian. *Liberté, égalité, fraternité!*"

He put his long-fingered hands together in light applause. "Genevieve, allow me to applaud your accent. Pure Parisian French, down to the little throaty trill."

"Uvular," she said. "I *did* teach French," she reminded him. "And I had a French grandmother."

"What was her name?"

"Michelle." She spoke without thinking. But there was no link. Only to her pen-name, and he didn't know that.

"Beautiful!" He gave a deep theatrical exhalation. "So is Genevieve French too? But your colouring is pure Celt."

"And yours is pure Norman," she retorted. "We all know the Normans were the bad guys in those days. Raven hair, coal-black eyes. The Norman invaders made an extensive penetration into Cornwall."

"They did. But going way back the Trevelyans were a French-speaking family," he revealed. "May I ask how the book's going?"

Her expression lightened, lost some of its strain. "It's going well. Not like work at all. I'm enjoying myself."

He stared down at her with sceptical eyes. "Is there really a book in it?"

"Of course there is!" she fired back. "But I need to know all the secrets."

"What secrets, exactly?" he asked, his tone deepening and darkening.

She shrugged a satin-clad shoulder. "There aren't too many families without secrets."

"You mean dysfunctional families?"

She shook her cascading hair back over her shoulders. "Unhappy families have the most riveting stories. Take the Kennedys. It was almost as though they were labouring under a hereditary curse."

"It seemed like it," he agreed. "I'm sorry our family can't deliver any curses just so you can write a bestseller, Ms Grenville. What *is* a ghost-writer anyway?" he asked with some humour. "You write reams of stuff, but no words actually appear on the paper?"

"I *have* written reams," she said. "Well, maybe not reams, but I've written a lot. You know as well as I do the reader wants to be drawn into a really good *story*. An exciting story. It's no use putting down a dry-as-ash account. There are things about your family, going back to your grandfather, that I'd like to explore further. Hester is a fascinating woman. I'm getting to understand her."

His laugh was brief. "We must be the only two left on the planet. But *what* are you digging for? That's the burning question."

Where is all this leading, Genevieve? The voice of caution broke in with a warning.

She heeded it. "Look, you must excuse me. I can't stand around chatting in my nightclothes."

"Is that what we were doing? Chatting?" he asked suavely.

"Perhaps you could give me an hour or two when it's convenient?" she suggested.

His manner appeared perfectly relaxed. "I don't keep any secrets, Genevieve."

"I think you do. I can feel the secrets gusting like the wind around us."

"Really? Psychic, are you? I should have guessed." His dark eyes glittered behind hooded lids.

"Another one of my accomplishments," she said airily. "I don't want to upset your theory, but what I actually came downstairs for was to grab a couple of painkillers from the first-aid cabinet. I have a headache." She'd *had* a headache. It had been miraculously cured by the bloodflow to her head. "I couldn't sleep. That's all. I've worked practically the *entire* weekend," she tacked on virtuously.

"Perhaps you were missing me?" There was real devilment in his mesmeric gaze. "I have a suggestion. Nothing to panic you." He held up a palm at the wariness that came into her face. "Have you tried a single malt Scotch?"

"I don't have a bottle stashed away in my room, if that's what you mean."

"But *I* do." He waved an arm. "I'm pointing to

my father's study, by the way. It mightn't be the *best* thing in the world to relax you and afterwards send you straight off into a blissful sleep, but sex is out of the question, is it not?"

Her heart rocked crazily. *Sex?* "I thought we'd made that plain enough?" She overcompensated for her shocked reaction by speaking sharply.

"We did." He bowed his head, his smile brushing her skin like silk. "So let's go. One nip and I promise you it'll work better than any painkiller."

"I think I'd better stick with the aspirin." Hester couldn't have said it in a haughtier or more repressive fashion.

Only he laughed.

She *sooo* liked the sound of his laugh.

"Let me offer reassurance, Genevieve," he said. "You're completely safe. I won't eat you. I might want to, but it won't happen—I promise. Your well-being is sacred to me while you're under my roof."

"I think you lie." The excitement had increased one hundredfold.

He caught her hand, further undermining her resistance. "I *don't* lie, Ms Grenville." A steely note came into his voice. "No harm will come to you from me. A man can be tempted without crossing the line."

"And what line would that be?" She knew she shouldn't be provocative, but her hand being held captive by his had set loose a torrent of sensations like sparkling water gushing from a great fountain. "More experiments?"

"Do shut up, Genevieve," he said gently, drawing her back along the passageway. "One nip and we'll go upstairs. You to your room. Me to mine. Though it's probably the hardest thing I've had to do all week." He said it like a joke. It *wasn't*. He had thought of her continually.

Genevieve had to trip along to keep up with him, the hem of her nightdress and her light robe flying around her. "For goodness' sake, Bret, isn't this inappropriate?"

He had never heard his name sound so good. "Come on, now. You're a grown woman. And one of the smartest women I've yet met."

"Smart? Your tone implies I'm also on the sly side."

He didn't answer, but pulled her inside the door of his father's study, shutting the door. "Highly intelligent, bilingual." He turned back to her. "Or do you speak other foreign languages? Nothing would surprise me."

"I'm tempted to take up Japanese," she said, taking the much needed opportunity to wrap her flyaway robe more firmly across her body. She wished for a safety pin. A big one. But she could hardly ask for one. "This is a magnificent study."

She was brought to a halt, dazzled by the bold masculine furnishings and the "inner sanctum" atmosphere. A large portrait of a very handsome man in his prime hung high behind the imposing red cedar desk. The walls had been panelled in the same glossy timber as the imposing desk. The valuable rug on the floor she thought was antique Sultanbad. There were lots of bronze-mounted bookcases—some holding trophies galore. This was one room Nori hadn't shown her into.

Her eyes were drawn back to the large canvas. The resemblance was obvious. The same extraordinary eyes. They blazed in the hard handsome face rather fiercely, Genevieve thought. There was strength and much arrogance there. It was not a kind face. "Your father?" she asked.

"Yes."

A too brief answer?

"A strikingly handsome man. You have a strong

look of him." At the same time Trevelyan was
very much *himself.* For one thing she knew he was
kind, and his expression lacked that slightly repel-
lent arrogance. She did think he could be fierce
if the occasion demanded it. "It must have been
a dreadful shock, his tragic premature death?"

He turned away. "Sometimes I think the re-
verberations will go on for ever. Take a chair,
Genevieve. I'll pour you a drink."

"Please, not bath-sized," she cautioned, sinking
into a dark green leather armchair and arrang-
ing her robe modestly across and around her. "I
actually *like* a fine single malt. Now and again, I
hasten to say."

Right now she was in need of something to calm
her leaping nerves.

"Here you are. Just a little water." He handed
her a crystal tumbler. "Drink up. You might as
well."

"Might as well what?" Her green eyes flashed
up at him.

He had already decided he liked sea-green eyes
the best of all. "Settle down, Genevieve," he said
mildly, resting back himself against the desk.

It gave him a powerful advantage. "I'll settle
when I'm back upstairs," she said, fortifying her-

self with a long sip. "Forgive me, when your pain is still raw, but have there been lesser tragedies on the station? It has a long colonial history. I haven't as yet found many, beyond the sometimes fatal accidents that happen on a working cattle station."

He downed his Scotch in a couple of gulps. "What exactly has Hester given you? I have to tell you this all started out just as a diversion for her. She's been lost in the years since she could no longer play. No matter what Derryl has to say—he's a real Philistine—Hester was a very fine pianist."

"I'm sure she was. I'm hoping she'll allow me to listen to her recordings."

"Only two we could salvage," he said. "They're now safe on CD. It *is* the digital age."

"And the sound is good?"

"As good as very expensive technicians could get it. I think you'll be impressed."

"I can see I'll have to work very hard on my technique," she said. "One fears comparisons with a fine pianist."

"What technique would that be?" There was a slightly cynical twist to his mouth. "How to seduce a man on sight? How to keep him tantalised?"

She swallowed so fast she choked, had to cough. "Excuse me?"

"Get your breath back," he urged kindly. "Try as I might I can't exactly trust you, Genevieve. The ghostwriter is a cover-up."

"Is it? Why, then, am I expending so much time and effort? You don't trust me. But I've accepted you the way you are. And don't laugh." She saw the amused mockery that flared across his striking face.

"I wasn't planning to," he lied. "Come along, Genevieve. Let me take your glass. Empty, I see."

"Lord knows you didn't give me much."

He laughed. "Just a therapeutic dose. Where do you keep your stash when you're at home?" He placed the two tumblers on the open lid of the cabinet.

Genevieve rose to her feet, feeling she had lost so much grip on the situation it had robbed her of her normal composure. "As if I'd tell *you*." Her robe securely wrapped around her like armour, she started to move to the door.

"Wait for me." Again the inbuilt voice of command. "I don't want you tripping over the hem of that ravishing nightgown."

He could do anything with his voice, she

thought. Command attention. Reduce her legs to jelly. She stood there, heart palpitating. The pace of events was incredible. No wonder she felt so stressed. "I had no idea you were such a maddening man. I thought you'd be remote—on the severe side."

"Well, you got *that* wrong." He reached out for her and turned her so her back was pressed against the door.

Genevieve heard the swift rise of her own exhalation. She stared up at him, making a great effort to control her voice. "You gave me your solemn promise, remember?"

"Yes, yes, I did." He put his hands flat to the door on either side of her, effectively keeping her contained.

All chance of escape was gone.

"But surely that was a solemn promise not to take you to my bed?" he asked. "Well, not until such time as I'm invited."

Instantly she felt her body break out in a fine dew of perspiration. His bed! His *king-sized* bed! His mouth on her. His hands on her, gliding all over her responsive body. His touch on her breasts. Just the thought had her long slender legs wilting like flower stalks beneath her. She'd had no idea that with the right man she could morph into a *voluptuous* woman, waiting…longing…yearning…for that man to take her.

"I said nothing about not giving you a good-night kiss." He was staring into her widened green eyes. "Again, therapeutic. We need to blot out that ex-fiancé who shall be nameless for ever. What exactly did he do wrong?"

Fiancé? What fiancé? She received more sexual stimulation from the sound of Trevelyan's voice than from *anything* Mark had ever done to or with her. "It's a long story," she murmured, in a strangely somnolent voice.

"I'm sure you have plenty of those."

"Don't we all?" Somehow she rallied. "*Your* ex-fiancé—*Liane*—wouldn't make allowances for experimental kisses. She's still madly in love with you. Very stupidly, she lost you. Why is that? The short version will do."

He moved a hand to brush her cheek, as though gauging her temperature. "Maybe I'll tell you eventually—but not tonight. So, should I be flattered? Why would you think *I* broke it off?"

"I know you did." She spoke with certainty.

"Ah, a beautiful magnolia-skinned woman, with rippling Titian hair and sea-green eyes, is clairvoyant as well. I'm sure Liane confided she became very tired of being, in her words, 'second best'."

"*Was* she?" she asked with a troubled note. "Would any woman have to take second place to Djangala and the Trevelyan business empire?"

"Let me find the woman first," he suggested, super-gently. He pushed a glowing strand of hair back into the rippling red-gold mass.

"Could I ask you to let me go?"

"You sound a bit afraid?"

"So should you be," she said.

"Why would a goddess need to be afraid, let alone *entreat*?" he asked. "Besides, you don't *want* me to let you go, Genevieve. I do know a little bit about women."

"You know nothing about *me*." A flash of spirit.

"Ah, but that's the puzzling thing. I feel I *do* know you," he said. "You're familiar to me somehow. Maybe since you're so spiritually accomplished you can explain that?"

Everything seemed to be unfolding in slow motion. The sense of intimacy confounded her. So much so Genevieve found it a huge effort just to keep breathing. "Maybe we met in another life?" she suggested. Her voice, even to her own ears, sounded *dreamy*. But that was the mesmerising effect his brilliant dark gaze was having on her. "Maybe we're kindred souls? Who knows?"

"Karma, perhaps? But how can you tell?"

He was staring down at her as if the answer lay in the shimmering depths of her eyes.

She turned her head to one side. "Are you trying to hypnotise me?"

"Do you think that might help us to understand what's going on here?" he asked.

"So you *are* trying to hypnotise me?"

His voice dropped low into his chest. "I might, if I didn't have to consider the *enormity* of it." He turned her face back to him. "You're here under my roof, hence under my protection. Headache gone?"

"Yes."

"Wow! That was quick."

She flared up at his changed tone. "I wasn't lying. I *did* have a headache."

"Miraculously cured."

Was his smile that left her throbbing with desire *triumphant*? "How you enjoy baiting me." She turned on him in accusation.

"Maybe I do, Genevieve. But my heart isn't really in it."

"You've got a heart, then?" If he didn't, she *had*.

"I must. It's hammering away. Like yours." Briefly he touched a hand to her breast, as if to check her heartbeat. "Anyway, I thought you wanted some excitement?" His breath was warm, spirit-flavoured against her cheek. "Isn't that what you said was needed? A bit of *excitement*?"

"Who would have thought it? You're a devil with women." Her iridescent eyes challenged.

"Nonsense." Very gently he moved his hands beneath the thick silky fall of her hair, encircling her nape. "The way I see it, Genevieve, you're definitely a witch—as stated."

She was trembling visibly, vibrations moving through her body. She wanted him to touch her breast again. How foolish was that? "I can't be. I don't twitch my nose." She tried for a joke. Anything to lighten the emotion-charged atmosphere.

They were both in some sort of sensual trance. Pressure was mounting. None of it of her choosing, she tried to excuse herself. There had been no rapid escalation of attraction. She had been visited by that most extraordinary of events. The *coup de foudre*. Love at first sight. The deed was done. No magic spell could undo it.

They continued to remain tantalising inches

apart. It was a distance Trevelyan felt committed to, astounded to find his habitual hard control was damn near fragile. He weakened to the extent that he allowed his questing mouth to trail down from her temple, across her heated cheek, finally taking and closing in on her luscious mouth.

Genevieve's whole body convulsed as his tongue slipped into her open mouth, tangling with hers after a single erotic split second. She felt engulfed in flames. Her nipples, already aroused, budded tight against the silk-satin of her gown. There was an urgent near-painful throbbing down low in her body. What was happening was *beyond* reason she thought.

He breathed her name.

Genevieve.

She couldn't be sure. It could have been her mind playing tricks on her. Her limbs felt so weak she felt the urgent need to lie down with him. She was drowning in an unprecedented rapture. It was even possible she would dissolve in her own tears. They were pricking her eyes.

Adrenalin was raging like volcanic lava through Trevelyan's veins, causing his heart to knock punishingly against his ribs. He wanted this woman so badly he would have had to be forged from steel to resist her. Yet he managed to hold on to sufficient strength, bolstered by his innate sense of responsibility, to realise that if he pulled her beautiful yielding body into him, fused her hard against him, he would lose himself and her in the bonfire.

Doing the right thing mattered. He had a duty to her. That wild, primitive part of him that she so easily called up like a great storm, that part that was *mad* to take her, had to be controlled. For both their sakes.

He gave it long moments, his hands clutching her delicate shoulders. When he spoke his voice had a rough edge. "What do you say? Enough excitement for the night?"

It was a worry, but she couldn't speak.

"You're a very sensual woman, Genevieve," he breathed, thinking it had to be the understatement of the year.

"So I'm to believe *I* initiated this?" Slowly she lifted her head. If his hands weren't clamped so firmly on her shoulders she felt she might slump to the floor.

"You are every man's dream." His voice was

still rough with control. "Your ex-fiancé must have been a perfect fool."

"I don't remember." How could she remember Mark when she was utterly exposed to Trevelyan?

"Let me get this straight. He didn't grovel? Beg for you to take him back?"

Her backbone straightened. "I wouldn't have taken him back if he'd prostrated himself on the floor, inviting me to stomp all over him."

He cut his laugh short. "I take it he betrayed you in some way?" He was closely watching her face.

"Trust counts," she said. No residual anger, just a plain statement of fact. "It's probably the most important thing between a man and a woman."

"You mean that?"

The seriousness of his tone had her searching his eyes. "Of course I mean it. I *do*."

"That sounded a bit like a marriage vow, Genevieve."

"Well, we all have to get married finally, don't we? I want children. I want the man I love to father them."

His lustrous eyes gleamed. "I'm not reading your need for a marriage proposal into this, am I, Genevieve?"

She forced herself to cast off the enveloping

veils of sexual languor. "I think it's about time we finished this conversation, don't you? Are you going to open the door?"

"Alas, alas, I must," he lamented, removing his hands from her shoulders. "I might wish we could stay here until dawn, but we both need our sleep."

When they were safely back in the corridor she said, "Before I leave I'd love to see the rock paintings. I understand they're in what you call the Hill Country?"

"Before you *leave*?" he queried, making it sound as if there was no possibility of that.

"Five or six months' time," she faltered, perturbed by his tone.

"Well, we'd better get cracking then," he said with a satirical edge. "I'll find time fairly soon. I can't promise when. The aerial muster comes first."

"You mean *you'll* take me?"

"You're not going to see them without me," he assured her dryly.

"Exactly what *I* thought."

"And one more thing," he called as she turned away to make her escape, the hem of her apricot robe spinning around her ankles.

"Yes?"

His dark gaze held her firmly in place. "Will you *want* to leave? That's the thing."

CHAPTER SEVEN

IT TURNED out to be a hectic week. Wonder of wonders, Hester had taken it into her head to approve the young woman who was ghostwriting her book.

Hester Trevelyan with Genevieve Grenville.

Genevieve could see it now. Hester's name in capitals, of course.

Hester spent several hours a day with Genevieve, imparting recently surfaced memories and more information. "I'm really pleased with the way you're working," she said, fingering her pearls. "You've organised everything into fine order."

"I think so too." No point in being unduly modest. She had worked very hard, not needing motivation.

"Dull bits out. Interesting bits in. Djangala has a ghost, you know."

Genevieve's heart leapt into her throat. "Man or woman?"

"A young woman speared to death many times by her wicked old husband," Hester said quite casually, as though spearing were an everyday affair. "Such violent creatures, men," she said derisively. "They behave like savages even when they're not. It was the same old story. A young man—the lover—died too. The *kurdaicha* man got him. It was the *kurdaicha* man's job to avenge the husband on the young man."

"So this is an aboriginal legend?" Genevieve asked, her heartbeat slowing.

"Legend nothing!" Hester sent her a sharp look. "The killings were real. There are strict rules. They were broken. The lovers knew what would overtake them, but they took the risk nevertheless. Lovers are forever doing that," she said harshly. "Lovers are the biggest risk-takers of all."

"So the speared young woman has been seen at various times around the station?"

"Not *around*," Hester exploded. "There is only *one* place. That is where my father found her body. Actually what was *left* of her body, what with all the birds and wildlife around."

"How horrible!" Genevieve shuddered. "So how does she appear—and where?"

"Everyone on the station knows where she appears. You're the only one who doesn't and I'm not about to enlighten you. You're a young woman with a great deal of imagination."

"But I'd like to put it in the book. Any other ghosts?" Genevieve looked directly into the old lady's eyes, wishing she could tap into Hester's secrets.

"We white people keep our ghosts corralled," Hester said dryly, in her turn studying Genevieve closely. "I'm not speaking in fun, my dear. This is serious business. Aborigines believe in sorcery and magical operations. Not so long ago on this very station the *kurdaicha* man was responsible for several deaths. Men and women who had broken jealously guarded taboos. If he was powerful enough he didn't have to creep up on them with his spear, he *sang* them to death. You can't question it. I assure you it happened."

"Even in the city one hears of such remarkable stories," Genevieve said. "The Outback has a mysticism and a glamour for we city-dwellers. Is it possible the person under the spell believed in it so implicitly it was broadly speaking suicide? Auto-suggestion? It works. Many people believe placebos work if the idea is firmly planted in their minds."

"There you go!" exclaimed Hester. "Anyway, it was a very long time ago."

"Is *anything* a long time ago?" Genevieve asked. "Aren't we all immersed in the past?"

Hester subjected her to a long fixed stare, then she leaned in. "You're a highly unusual young woman." She tapped Genevieve sharply on the back of the hand. "I don't expect comments like that from someone your age. Mine, certainly. But *you*?"

"That's my mindset. I studied philosophy at university."

"Ah, the great minds!" Hester exclaimed. "I have to tell you I've been grappling with life's most fundamental questions for donkey's years now. I know no more now than I did then. In my view even the most brilliant minds didn't get it right. Now, enough of that! I've put my hand on some old photographs we might be able to use."

"Let's see them," Genevieve responded with keen interest. "You really were remarkably beautiful, Ms Trevelyan." It was no stretch of the truth.

The expression on Hester's face didn't change with the compliment, as sincerely as it had been meant. "Didn't have a beautiful *heart*," she said with what sounded like self-loathing. "Much less soul. I wasn't a good person. The years haven't improved me. I know what people think of me. They want me to die. Not Bret. Bret knows me better than anyone. You don't find men like Bret."

No argument there.

Genevieve began to sort through the faded photographs, offering up a silent prayer that she would find Catherine in at least one of them. Not prominently featured, perhaps, but a figure in a group?

When she finally came on a surprisingly clear photograph of a large group of guests she could barely make a sound or utter a word. Most were smiling at the camera, a few had been caught off guard, one was grimacing in the sun.

Hester, expecting a different reaction, looked at her in amazement, brows fiercely knotted. "What's wrong with you, girl? You've gone quite pale."

Genevieve had a struggle to find her voice. "The heat, I expect. I'm not used to it."

"You looked as cool as a cucumber a moment ago," Hester said with some scepticism but real concern. "So what caught your eye?"

"A p-particular face, I suppose," Genevieve stammered. "A lovely face. Who's that?" She turned the black and white photograph towards Hester.

For an instant Hester turned to a pillar of stone. Then, galvanised, she grabbed the photograph out of Genevieve's hand with no apology for her rudeness. "This one shouldn't be here." Her voice was reedy with strain.

"It was stuck behind one of the others, but it's a photograph that should be included, don't you think? Who is the lovely blonde standing beside you? You're resting your hand on her shoulder. You look so happy."

The petite dark-haired young woman on Catherine's left was smiling broadly. It had to be Patricia. A rather formidable-looking young woman to Hester's right was staring off into the distance.

Hester's forehead had broken out into a damp sweat. "You're right. It is hot. I need to go back to my room. Carry on without me."

"May I have the photograph back?" Genevieve dared to ask.

"*No!*" Hester Trevelyan barked. "I don't want *anyone* to see her."

But I have seen her.

The lovely blonde was Catherine. Her mouth was tilted in a carefree smile, her beautiful hair was caught back with a scarf, a silky flap falling on her shoulder. Genevieve recognised Hester's hand on her shoulder as proprietorial.

Genevieve had the absolute certainty that Catherine was the young woman Hester had loved. No doubts at all. A voice had been continually whispering in her ear since she'd arrived on Djangala. Catherine dead for decades but still *here*. Hester had loved Catherine, but for some reason come to hate her. Was it conceivable both brother *and* sister had fallen in love with Catherine? It wasn't that unusual. And what of Patricia? The woman in waiting? If it was a love triangle it had an entirely different configuration from her initial conventional beliefs.

Love and hate were different sides of the same coin. She could see now her initial preconceptions would have to be jettisoned.

A few mornings later, Nori came at a near rush into the library. The expression on her normally serene face was somewhat rattled.

"Well, what is it?" Hester cranked her snow-white head about like a highly irritable cockatoo.

Hester had to be going for the world record for rudeness, Genevieve thought. Maybe she had it already? Or was Hester's abrasive manner so long entrenched it could be the result of the self-loathing she had so briefly glimpsed?

"I thought you would want to know, Ms Trevelyan, Ms Rawleigh has flown in," Nori explained.

"What through the *door*?" Hester's voice came close to an enraged squawk.

Genevieve's own intense interest in the morning's proceedings was spoiled. Liane Rawleigh! She was no happier to hear that than Hester.

"One of the men brought the message. A helicopter dropped Ms Rawleigh off. She is staying over, perhaps?"

"Damn and blast!" Hester looked as if she wanted to commit murder. "I wonder what she wants?" she asked wrathfully. "I suppose the simplest explanation is she wants Bret. I'm most unpleasantly put out, I can tell you. What that young woman did still comes back to me. I never did like her. Moreover, I don't wish to deal with her."

She staggered up, as majestically as she could, looking down at the seated Genevieve.

"You will have to take care of it, my dear. Not that she will stay in the house long," she commented acidly. "She'll be chasing after Bret. If she asks where he is, don't tell her. It gladdens my heart to know she'll never get him back. Not in a million years. I don't know how they got together in the first place. Proclivity, I suppose, and that pushy mother of hers. Why, they don't even speak the same language! Liane Rawleigh was simply not good enough for my great-nephew. I'm going to my room. You can send up tea, Mrs Cahill. I'll have lunch in my room as well. Dinner too, if she's staying over. God forbid for a few days. I'm off!" she announced, as though she was about to lead an expedition into the Interior. "Genevieve, I put you in charge."

Nori remained in the library for a few moments after Hester had stalked off, listing to one side. "For once I agree with Ms Trevelyan," she said.

"Liane is *not* popular?"

"If it's possible she's even more odious to me than Ms Hester," Nori confessed.

"Why tolerate it?" Genevieve asked, angry on Nori's account.

"You know the old saying—softly, softly, catchee monkey?" Nori smiled.

"And you've turned the gentle approach into an art form." Genevieve smiled back. "No one seems to know where the phrase came from. Some say Baden-Powell, the founder of the Boy

Scouts, during his time in West Africa. Others think it's Chinese. Whatever it's origin, caution is very good advice."

Nori looked conflicted. "Ms Trevelyan told us not to tell her where Bret is if she asks. Perhaps we should?" She looked to Genevieve to decide.

"Well, I don't *know*, do I?"

"Steven spoke of Camp Five," Nori offered tentatively.

"Look, let her go in search." Genevieve took less than a few seconds to make a decision. "I've a feeling she'll find him wherever he is."

An impish smile curved Nori's lips. "You forget my husband will warn him."

Less than ten minutes later Liane strode purposefully into the house, pushing with her usual arrogance past Nori, who had greeted her at the door.

"I'm after Bret." She spoke in her clear piercing voice. "It's fairly urgent. Did he say where he and the men would be working today?"

"I'm so sorry, Ms Rawleigh. I have no idea."

"I'll find him." Liane chopped Nori off. "Where is Ms Grenville? Surely you know *that*?"

"In the library." Nori felt confident Gena could handle such an abrasive person.

"No tea for me," Liane called, although tea had not been offered. "I'll have a word with Ms Grenville, then I'll be off. Where's Ms Trevelyan, by the way?"

Nori suddenly saw a way to spare Gena too much of Liane's company. "She will be downstairs shortly," she fibbed.

"Then I won't be here."

In the library Genevieve awaited Trevelyan's ex-fiancée's entrance. Another bumpy conversation? She sat at ease, playing with the pen in her hand.

"What? Nothing to do?" Liane dispensed with civilities.

"Plenty to do. Just taking a break."

"You don't happen to know where Bret is?" Liane was making no attempt to be friendly.

Genevieve shook her head. "Sorry. I wouldn't know."

"Of course you wouldn't," Liane said after a moment's consideration. "I can't believe you've hung in this long. Hester must be the ultimate slavedriver."

"Actually, we get along like a house on fire," Genevieve said.

Liane bit off a laugh. "Come on, Ms Grenville. I'm not a fool."

"Did I suggest you were? Ms Trevelyan is a very interesting woman. We have much in common."

"Like that dreadful old maid's bun." Liane gave a disparaging laugh, running a hand over her long glossy dark hair, tied back with a silk scarf. She looked great in riding gear, down to the glossy boots, a cream akubra in her hand. All set to chase after Trevelyan, in fact.

"I think the term 'old maid' is politically incorrect." Genevieve sat back, pondering the issue. "Many women remain unmarried by choice. Others have tragedies in their lives, or responsibilities as carers to a family member or invalid parents, that prevent them from taking the step of marriage. There's no call to be rude either. Now, I must get on," she said, borrowing Hester's autocratic manner. "Ms Trevelyan will be joining me shortly."

"Better you than me." Liane took to her heels— a woman who couldn't get away fast enough.

Her dreams were back. She was always in peril. This vivid dreaming had started shortly after she had lost her mother. Maybe a learned psychotherapist who had years of experience could explain it all to her. Her dreams reflected her unresolved grief and her insecurities, perhaps? Logical enough, yet she knew explanations wouldn't help. Nor would they stop the dreams. They happened—like her *moments*. She couldn't shut the door on them. She had no choice. Perhaps her over-active imagination wasn't satisfied with her writing alone?

That night she had to shake herself awake. She pressed her hands to her eyes, then lifted herself up on one elbow. Moonlight was streaming into her room. It was an extraordinarily beautiful night. So *light*! She could almost see the two shadowy figures at the end of her bed. They didn't frighten her. Rather, the shapes caught in the silver-white radiance embraced her, calming her.

She had been dreaming of Catherine. Nothing strange about that, as Catherine was in the forefront of her mind. What was unusual was that Catherine in her dream had had a companion—another fair-haired young woman. Their arms had been linked, as if they were friends. She'd seen them as clearly as they had her. Only as she'd called to them they'd begun to walk away from her, taking an upward path. The landscape was like the dark, disturbing backgrounds da Vinci had sometimes employed in his paintings. Genevieve had recognised the wild bush. At the foot of the steep incline was a stream, raging over rocks, carrying debris.

The dream still held her fast, frame after frame. She felt anxiety...dread... A name kept repeating itself, yet she couldn't hear clearly enough to make it out, though she strained and strained. Was it Cat? Catherine?

Snap out of it, Genevieve. Snap out of it.

It was a familiar ritual, this self-admonition to bring her out of her troubling dreams. Some people had pleasant dreams—a rehash of events in their lives. Others had no memory of their dreams. Why was *she* the way she was? God knew. She couldn't command her dreams, even though she craved a good night's sleep. And any attempt to interpret or understand her dreams she had long since abandoned.

Only this one had been different. Catherine and the other young woman had been trying to tell her something.

What?

It would come to her if she didn't force it. Perhaps when she awoke in the morning the message would come intact into her mind. She had often tried to no avail to recall a name in the night, only to have the name pop into her mind the instant she woke up. The brain, the greatest computer of them all, had been searching all night.

She awoke with a shock, for a moment not knowing where she was. Dawn was sifting into her room in a luminous mist. Down in the garden a bird was singing its heart out. Thousands of other voices would soon join it. The ritual dawn chorus—the warbling of the wild. Now she knew she was on Outback Djangala. It was imperative she get up immediately. Go looking for Trevelyan. Hopefully he hadn't yet left the homestead, although she knew he started his long days at dawn. The name that had been buried in her subconscious had come instantly into her waking mind.

Kit. Christopher.

Christopher Wakefield was Sondra's grieving husband.

She was meant to understand that Kit Wakefield was falling into the abyss. His grief over the tragic violent death of his young wife loomed so large in his life it was oppressing him to the extent he felt there was no point in going on.

She rushed along the corridor, down the steps,

her long red-gold hair whipping behind her. No time to dress properly. She had pulled a pale green caftan with gold embroidery over her head. No shoes either. All she knew was she had been given a responsibility. That responsibility was to tell Trevelyan. He was the one who would act.

Miracles of miracles, he hadn't left the homestead. He was standing at the front door. Liane was with him. She appeared to be arguing strenuously with him about something. Genevieve hadn't gone downstairs for dinner the previous evening to join them, claiming she had too much to do. She had settled for a tray in her room. As had Hester.

"Bret!" she cried out, desperate to gain his attention.

He swung to see her slender body in fluid motion. The loose garment she was wearing clung to its contours as if she was wearing nothing beneath it. She appeared to him like some inspirational figure out of a beautiful painting. Immediately he was impelled to go to her, feeling a sense of alarm. What was it she wanted? The urgency in her beautiful face was plain enough.

"Genevieve, what's wrong?"

"It's not me," she panted, "but I have something

to tell you. Something to pass on." Up close to him now, she sought and held his eyes.

"Is she for *real*?" Liane demanded hotly from behind them, outraged by Genevieve's extraordinary appearance—and at this hour! The supposed ghostwriter had undergone a highly unwelcome transformation. And that pre-Raphaelite hair! Who *was* this Genevieve Grenville? What was she up to? Liane's eyes took on a hard light. Time to check this ghostwriter out.

Genevieve placed an urgent hand on Trevelyan's arm. "I had a dream—"

"God, not Martin Luther King?" Liane burst out in scorn.

Genevieve looked back almost blindly at the scornful face. "It was a young woman in his campaign office who actually said, 'I have a dream'. King took it up." With relief, she turned back to Trevelyan. "Kit Wakefield is in trouble," she told him, as she was meant to. "I fear he's suicidal."

A long swathe of glorious hair was coiled around her throat. Trevelyan found himself reaching out to loosen it. His answer was gentle enough, but mixed with caution and concern. "Genevieve, you don't even *know* Kit."

"Sondra told me."

Behind them Liane let out an angry bark of laughter. She was shocked and alarmed by Trevelyan's hand on Genevieve's hair. "You talk to ghosts, do you? I repeat—are you for *real*?"

Genevieve spun so the loose sleeves of her silk caftan billowed like wings. "Who's to say what's real and what isn't? Not *you*!"

"I beg your pardon?" Liane was genuinely taken aback. "The consensus of opinion among those with their heads screwed on is there are *no* ghosts," she said, with biting sarcasm.

"Not everyone adheres to that." Genevieve concentrated her attention on Trevelyan—the only one who mattered. "She came to me in a dream. I often dream. I have good reasons to trust my dreams."

"Oh, this is too much!" Liane groaned. "I could throw up."

Trevelyan turned on her. "We can only hope you won't match the deed to the words."

Liane almost danced in her fury. "Bret, you *can't* let this lunacy go by. You really ought to pack her off home. Clearly she's unbalanced."

Genevieve barely heard the interruption. "He needs you *today*." She stared with great intensity into Trevelyan's dark eyes. "*Trust me.* I'll pack up and leave if I'm wrong."

"Is that a promise?" Liane shouted.

Both Trevelyan and Genevieve ignored her. "You have real fears for his life?" Trevelyan asked, without any discernible note of scepticism.

"*Sondra* fears for his life," she corrected.

There was fierce anger in Liane's face. "God, I have to pinch myself hard. You're not listening to her, are you, Bret? She's a nutcase."

"We all have fears for Kit," said Trevelyan.

"Not *me*!" Liane uttered harshly. "He wasn't in love with her anyway. Kit has always loved *me*."

Trevelyan rounded on her. "Is it always going to be too late for you to wake up, Liane? Kit fell out of love with you long ago. He married Sondra. They were happy."

Liane's ice-blue eyes grew bright with rage. "I know better."

"Stop now, Liane," he warned. "It won't hurt to take the helicopter over. Do you want to come?" he asked Genevieve, excluding Liane. "I'll give you three minutes to get dressed."

Genevieve took off on winged feet, her ears blocking out Liane Rawleigh's spiralling cries of protest.

* * *

Trevelyan set the helicopter down as light as a bird on a greenish-brown patch of lawn. They had scouted the relatively small Wakefield spread from the air. No sign of human life. Cattle sitting in the shade of the trees. Six or seven brumbies, running like the wind. Emu mothers and chicks trotting in procession.

They were now approaching the large timber homestead—a pleasing building with a broad front verandah. "Stay behind me," Trevelyan said. "I'll check the house out first."

What marred the scene was its air of abandonment, the desolation that hung over the house and grounds. A fairly extensive garden that once would have flourished was now withered and forlorn, except for a solitary yellow rosebush that defied the odds and continued to produce beautiful blooms. Sondra would have been the gardener, Genevieve thought. Such blooming was a small miracle in itself. Her mind was continuing to make connections. Irrational, maybe, but she stooped to pluck a perfect yellow bud. The petals gave off an exquisite perfume.

Trevelyan called Kit Wakefield's name. No answer. He took the short flight of steps onto the porch at a leap and tried the door. It was open.

He pushed it back against the wall, shouting Kit's name. If he was anywhere in the vicinity he should have heard.

"Where they hell to begin, then?" he muttered to himself.

"He's in the house," a voice said softly.

Genevieve had come up behind him.

"Ah, Genevieve!" There was no clear reason for any of this, but he was following her lead as if impelled.

"I didn't make the decision," Genevieve read his mind. "The decision was made for us. We have to find him."

They did find Kit Wakefield. He was lying on the double bed in the main bedroom, his long thin body turned away from them. There was a letter propped against the alarm clock on the nearest bedside table. A twenty-two rifle was leaning against the wardrobe. Alarm washed through Trevelyan, although he knew at once the rifle hadn't been put to use. *Yet.* The dry, stale air was heavy with the smell of alcohol.

"Go outside, Genevieve," Trevelyan said over his shoulder. "Wait on the porch."

"Please, I'm all right here." She didn't want to go away. She had to stay.

Trevelyan didn't bother to argue. He knew she wouldn't go. He put his arm on the young man's shoulder and shook him violently. He desperately needed a response.

"Kit!" He leant over the bed, shouting in Kit Wakefield's ear. "Come on, Kit. Wake up. It's me, Bret."

Wakefield didn't stir. Then, after a few silent heartbeats, he articulated one badly slurred word. "Bret?"

"Yes, it's me, man. Wake up," Trevelyan ordered forcefully. "We need to talk."

Kit didn't answer.

"Go find a bucket and fill it with water." Trevelyan gave Genevieve the order.

"Shouldn't be hard to find one."

She was back within moments. Trevelyan took the brimming bucket from her, then pitched the entire contents over the figure on the bed.

This time Kit reacted. He threw himself over onto his back, panting, spitting, spluttering madly, "Oo! Did you have to do that?" he croaked. There was a note like betrayal in his voice. It was clear he had wanted to be alone to do whatever he had intended to do.

"You bet your life I did," Trevelyan responded

vigorously. "What's going on here, Kit? What the hell is in that note? I see it's addressed to me."

"You're the top bloke, Bret," Kit mumbled. "Who else?"

He looked ghastly, Genevieve thought. His light brown curly hair was dark with sweat, and badly tousled—as if he hadn't brushed it for days on end. His half-open shirt exposed his ribcage. His ribs were so close to the surface they were almost breaking through the skin. He had badly blood-shot eyes, and he was extremely pale considering he lived and worked on the desert fringe.

"Kit, you're not acting like the man I know you are," Trevelyan said rousingly. "I understand your grief, but you've got people who care about you."

"No Sondra." Kit was totally unable to hide his unrelenting grief. It had drained him of the will to go on.

What Genevieve did next was instinctive. She moved from behind Trevelyan's tall figure that had partially blocked her, joining him at the bed-side. "Sondra doesn't want you to die, Kit," she said, with all the persuasiveness she could muster. "She wants you to live."

Kit Wakefield stared back at her with a kind of stunned dismay. "What are you telling me?

Who are you anyway? An angel?" His bloodshot eyes moved sharply to Trevelyan. "Who *is* this woman?"

"She's with me. She's staying at Djangala."

Kit broke in on him. "You think because of *that*—?" He sat up, groaning, startled into action.

"I trust her," Trevelyan said with finality. "There are times one has to put one's trust in someone without understanding why. I've always relied on my instincts—especially when I feel there's danger. Genevieve had a very vivid dream with Sondra in it. She was saying your name, over and over. When Genevieve woke this morning she knew she had to do something. She did the right thing. She came to me."

"A dream? You *saw* Sondra? But I don't know you. You never met Sondra," Kit protested, clearly distressed.

"I knew her in my dream," Genevieve said. "She had long blonde hair. She was very visible. She wanted me to tell you she wants you to live." Genevieve leaned over, placing the yellow rose-bud in Kit Wakefield's nerveless hand. "You have to look your grief in the face. This is what she wants."

"God!"

Kit Wakefield thrust one desperate hand through his knotted hair. His right hand, however, clung to the yellow rose that showed no sign of wilting in the heat.

"Sondra doesn't want me to die?"

He stared back at Genevieve as though she just might be a heavenly visitation. She was certainly different from anyone he had ever known. More significantly, Bret trusted her.

"Sondra sent us here, Kit," Trevelyan said. Whether it was making sense or not—and surely it *couldn't* be—Kit was definitely responding, Trevelyan thought. "What I want you to do is get up, shower and shave, throw a few things in a bag. We'll make you some strong coffee, then I'm taking you back to Djangala for a little R&R. You look awful, by the way," he said with a bracing smile. "It's like I said, Kit. You have friends."

Trevelyan put out a hand, placing it rather solemnly on Genevieve's shoulder.

"I have to thank you, Genevieve," he said. "It would appear you're the chosen one."

CHAPTER EIGHT

GENEVIEVE found herself warming more and more to her project, despite her underlying motive for taking on the job. And Hester, though she didn't make an appearance if she was in pain, was slowly becoming a more agreeable person. She had even dropped the "Mrs Cahill" with Nori, following Genevieve's lead.

"You're a miracle-worker, Gena," Nori confided, her heart lightened.

"I'm certainly not that." Genevieve shrugged it off. "But I try to understand. If a person isn't blessed with love, understanding has to be a help—don't you think?"

Nori agreed. Genevieve had been instrumental in bringing about Ms Trevelyan's most welcome sea change.

In the end, it was the old photograph that did it. Hester was becoming more involved in their project, viewing Genevieve with respect, even a degree of affection.

"I do enjoy your company, my dear," she said, as she finished off a potful of hot sweet tea. She was seated at an angle to Genevieve's desk. "You're a born storyteller. It's as though you're seeing it all through *my* eyes."

Genevieve's coffee lay untouched near her hand. "You won't tell me about that lovely blonde in the photograph?" She knew she was diving headfirst into possible trouble.

Hester's eyes seemed to sink more deeply into their sockets. "There's only so much I can speak about, Genevieve."

"It upsets you?" Genevieve asked gently.

Hester turned the words over in her mind, weighing them up. "I'll have to speak to Bret," she said finally. "If he's against including an old sad story, that's it, my dear. Some things are better not put down on paper."

"You can *speak* about it, then?" Genevieve asked quietly. "If you and Bret don't want a particular event or story included, then that's it!"

"*You* should ask him," Hester said, frowning in concentration. "I sense he's strongly drawn to you."

"I've done nothing to warrant it." Genevieve only just managed to conceal her shock.

"My dear, you don't have to *do* anything," Hester remarked, very dryly. "We're either drawn to people or we're not. I can understand it, of course. You're a beautiful, highly intelligent young woman, with good manners. The Queen's late mother, the Dowager Queen Elizabeth, was once asked what quality she thought most necessary to get us smoothly through life. Her answer was *good manners*. I have to say I've been a tad short on them. Pain, grief… They take you down to dark places. By the way, Bret told me *you* were instrumental in getting young Wakefield to stay with us. As good as saved his life! I have to say Kit's looking a whole lot better since he arrived. Bret has done the right thing, setting him to work. The men will look out for him. Everyone likes Kit Wakefield. But losing the love of your life is a tremendous blow. Poor little Sondra—rest her soul. She didn't deserve to die like that. The most dreadful things happen to good people. The bad seem to get off scot-free."

No one got off entirely scot-free, Genevieve thought. And her objective remained: to find out where exactly everyone had been the day catastrophe had come to her kinswoman Catherine.

* * *

Trevelyan pushed his leather chair away from his desk so forcibly it smacked into a cabinet. He was trying to calm a rising anger that held a bitter tang and a certain sense of disappointment. Someone had sent him a book—no inscription, no covering note—freighted in with the usual station supplies.

The fact the book had surfaced wasn't strange. It had been bound to happen. He knew who had sent it. Liane had left Djangala in a jealous rage.

In the early days he had never guessed at Liane's true nature. Why would he have? She had always been at her best with him. Until such time as he was away on an extended overseas business trip, that was.

This was the result of a woman's jealousy. As for him—all doubts and speculations were over.

It was a beautifully produced hardback copy of Michelle Laurent's *Secrets of the Past*. The cover design featured a beautiful young blonde woman. There was a well-known magazine's sticker affixed to the top right hand corner: *Great Read*. The back cover offered information about the author, along with a photograph of her.

So why was he surprised he *wasn't* surprised?

There were several reasons. He hadn't trusted Genevieve or her motivation from the start. And his hunches were nearly always right. Michelle Laurent was Genevieve Grenville's pen-name. He recalled how she had told him about her grandmother Michelle. Michelle had been French. But the book was an achievement—so why the big mystery?

Genevieve appeared to have a passion for secrets. Hester had hinted that Genevieve had shown interest in the old tragedy of Catherine Lytton. She was leaving it to him to decide whether he wanted the heavy cloak of silence that had been drawn over the incident to remain.

The key question was: why was Genevieve Grenville, published author, so deeply interested in that particular old story? Why had she come to Djangala, complete with a covering disguise? Was it possible she had some family connection to Catherine Lytton? Far more likely she wanted to gather material and write another bestseller based on a true-life tragedy on Djangala station. He supposed that was natural for writers seeking out inspiration.

What he had to do now was unmask her; get to the bottom of things. He hated all this subterfuge, but he had no intention of confronting her tonight, though he dearly wanted to. She had succeeded in getting Hester's permission to play one of Hester's old CDs after dinner. Derryl might take off after ten minutes or so, but Kit, a music lover, had expressed a desire to hear the recording too. And, as promised, he had organised to take Genevieve on an exploratory trip to the Hill Country the following afternoon.

The confrontation would have to wait until then. Genevieve Grenville—aka Michelle Laurent—who thought she could delve at will into dark crevices, was as of now exposed.

It was a pity, in its way. Hester—notoriously hard on people—liked her. And Genevieve, from all accounts, was doing a fine job. Why ever not? She was a published author. Also, in her mysterious way she had rescued Kit from a heart-rending fate, though she continued to insist her actions had been motivated by another party: Sondra. What was that? Telepathic communication from beyond the grave? He wasn't into psychic phenomena, but there was no question she was extraordinarily percipient. A whole hidden world lay behind Genevieve's sparkling, crystal-clear eyes.

What *was* she? he asked himself. Halfway between woman and witch?

* * *

Blessing or burden, Genevieve's sixth sense told her she was out of favour with Trevelyan. There was no hint of challenge, much less even the slightest degree of hostility in his manner. He was himself. Only she *knew*. The microcurrents that ran swiftly between them if not visible were palpable.

She had imagined herself safe. Now she knew she wasn't. And the one to blame for the abrupt change was most likely Liane Rawleigh. She had made the huge mistake of arousing the green-eyed monster in Liane. Before she'd left Djangala Liane had as good as given herself away, leaving Genevieve with the disturbing thought Liane, with her eyes like chips of blue ice, was set on having her checked out. She supposed if someone was committed to the job the threads wouldn't be all that hard to pick up. Liane wouldn't have to do it herself. She could leave any checks to a private investigator. She wouldn't put it past her.

Whatever Liane had seen pass between her and Trevelyan, the quality of their exchanges must have presented a dire threat to Liane, who still had hopes of winning her ex-fiancé back. If looks could have killed, Genevieve would have considered herself in extreme danger. There were even links between what had happened to Catherine and what could happen to her if she ever found herself in a bad situation with Liane Rawleigh. Love could be a battlefield. The aim of war was to destroy the enemy.

Kit Wakefield, in the fortnight he had been staying at the homestead, working along with the station's stockmen during the day, was showing a marked improvement both in general health and demeanour. It was as though he was coming to terms with his grief and internalising it, locking his Sondra away in the caverns of his heart. He would always love her, but he appeared to have accepted that life went on and he had to go with it.

Genevieve he had come to look on as a real friend, who cared about what had happened to Sondra and what happened to him. Indeed, they'd had a couple of private conversations about Genevieve's extraordinary dream.

"Millions of people believe in an afterlife," Kit had mused. "There may not be proof positive, but it doesn't douse the fire of faith. My Sondra was a spiritual person."

Genevieve already knew that. She was grateful neither Trevelyan nor Kit had rejected her claim out of hand. It was obvious to them Genevieve truly believed—even if they couldn't grasp it—that she had been chosen to pass on Sondra's message. That apparently meant everything to Kit Wakefield. The difference between living and opting out of life.

After dinner Hester retired to her suite, saying she had no wish to stay and listen to her long past performances. All the same, she had given her consent to Genevieve to have a practice hour here and there. On such occasions Genevieve had stuck religiously to the Tausig finger exercises. Maybe along the way she would pick a minor work from the stack of piano music in the piano seat. She had no wish to upset Hester or cause her pain.

She mightn't have thought it possible only a month ago, but she and Hester had settled into a good relationship that went beyond employer-employee. Hester had told Trevelyan that Genevieve was a great help to her. This provoked renewed bouts of speculation on Genevieve's part.

Hester had loved Catherine. Genevieve had the sense Hester was still genuinely bereft decades later. Which caused her to have serious doubts. Hester would not have harmed Catherine. And if not Hester, which of them had? Just because people didn't look dangerous, it didn't mean they weren't. Murderers appeared quite normal in their photographs. All that was needed was perceived threat.

The other alternative was, despite all the promptings that came from beyond her, it *had* been a tragic accident. Not a cover-up.

As expected, Derryl bade them goodnight after a bare fifteen minutes, although the opening of Liszt's "Mephisto Waltz" had Genevieve catching her breath.

She was amazed by Hester's breathtaking technique. It became apparent over the following most loved and difficult concert pieces that, virtuosity was her great strength. Technique and driving power. As the music filled the room Genevieve found herself longing to hear more of the fabled "singing" tone, a deeper lyricism—especially with the Schumann and Chopin.

She gave herself a mental shake. This was a wonderful performance. She was being far too critical. That was the trouble with being a trained musician. Instead of simply listening and enjoying, as Kit Wakefield clearly was, her ear was committed to studying the various interpretations in detail. She was familiar with every selection. Therefore it seemed to her that Hester at that stage had found her virtuoso technique but not the *passion*. Which begged the question. When exactly had she met Catherine? It was imperative to find out.

All the time his great-aunt's music had been playing Trevelyan's brilliant black eyes had rested on Genevieve's expressive face. He could see plainly the playing didn't seem quite right to her, though God knew Hester could have had a concert career if she'd persisted. Performances were such subjective things. It all depended on the point of view. He remembered his mother's playing. She had lacked Hester's superb technique, but she had something he thought Hester hadn't. *Soul*.

When the recording was finished, Kit put his hands together in loud applause. "That was splendid!" He turned to them, his thin face alive with pleasure. "I had no idea Miss Hester was such a marvellous pianist."

"And what do *you* think, Genevieve?" Trevelyan asked smoothly.

Her nerves were quivering and humming like a bow stroke across strings. "I agree with Kit.

That was a wonderful performance. Hester had a formidable technique."

"And?"

She knew she flushed. Had he reached the stage where he could read her mind? "I wish I had it. I think it so sad she had to be crippled with arthritis. Her music would have been such a comfort to her."

"Of course it would, "Kit agreed. "Sondra and I always thought it the greatest tragedy Jacqueline du Pré contracted multiple sclerosis. So many sad things happen in life…" His voice trailed off.

Trevelyan decided to stir things up. "Feel up to playing something for us, Genevieve?" He was deliberately putting her on the spot. But he played his hunch. She was an accomplished pianist.

"After *that* performance?" Genevieve endeavoured to cry off. She had never and could never reach Hester's daunting level of virtuosity

"You play too, Gena?" Kit turned to her in pleased surprise. "I'd love to hear you."

"We promise not to be too demanding," Trevelyan said suavely. "Hester tells me you've been getting in some practice. She would have stopped you if she hadn't approved."

Genevieve reacted to the suavity of his tone.

"All I got round to was exercises from my days at the Con. I'm sure you don't want to hear *them*."

Kit was taking stock of the flying sparks. "Play whatever you think we'd enjoy, Gena," he broke in. "If you studied at the Conservatorium you must know lots of pieces?"

"Very well." She picked up the gauntlet Trevelyan had thrown down.

Gracefully she walked to the nine-foot concert grand. She had played one often in the old days, property of the Conservatorium, and her father had presented her with a six-foot Steinway on her twenty-first birthday—a replacement for their ageing Bechstein.

She considered playing two Debussy *arabesques*—lovely, dreamy music—but as Trevelyan had more or less forced a performance on her she decided at the last minute to play her old party piece from her student days—Chopin's "Revolutionary Etude". It was a marvellously stirring *étude* in a set dedicated to his friend Franz Liszt. She knew fellow students had found the long, rapid harmonic minor scales that needed to be taken by the left hand extremely difficult, but the desire was growing in her to return fire and shake Trevelyan up. He was hiding it supremely well, but she knew he was angry with her. She would soon find out the reason for the sudden gulf.

Trevelyan rose to his feet. "You want the lid up?"

"Yes, thank you. One doesn't play with the lid down unless accompanying someone. And even then the lid would be opened a fraction."

"Forgive me. I stand corrected," he said suavely.

She knew she would pay for that. She sat down, made herself comfortable, then said over her shoulder to Kit, "Chopin's 'Revolutionary Etude'. You will know it, Kit. The 'Revolutionary' was the last piece played on free Polish radio before Poland was invaded by Germany. Chopin poured all his emotions into this *étude*. Sometimes it's called 'Etude on the Bombardment of Warsaw by the Russians'. I'll try to do it justice."

"Oh, bravo!" Kit looked brightly at Bret, who had resumed his seat. Bret's striking face was full of a certain amusement, and something else Kit couldn't quite define. It seemed to him there was some sort of contest going on between Trevelyan and Gena.

Genevieve began as she must if she was to do Chopin justice. *Passionately. Allegro con fuoco.*

Fast with fire. She played it to make Trevelyan shiver. Give Kit renewed heart.

When she was finished, throwing up her hands after the final chords, they were all astonished to see Hester, in a fantastic beribboned night garment loaded down with lace, moving from beneath the great archway into the living room.

"Play something else," she ordered in a gruff voice. Impossible to tell whether she was pleased or highly dismissive of Genevieve's gift.

Trevelyan didn't intervene. Instead he went to his great-aunt, leading her to a comfortable armchair.

"Go on. Go on," Hester ordered in a merciless tone, cocking her white head to one side the better to evaluate. "It doesn't matter what you play. I don't care," she said. Then immediately contradicted herself. "*Widmung.* Devotion. Schumann," she barked. "*Du meine Seele, du mein Herz.* You are my soul, my heart. Rapture. Peace, glimpses of heaven. He wrote it for his beloved Clara. Liszt arranged the piano solo. The music's there, if you can't play it from memory. Someone once told me I had to fall in love before I could successfully play *Widmung*," Hester abruptly confessed, further astonishing them. What would Hester say if the floodgates opened up? "I gave my everything to mastering all the technical details, you understand? At that time I didn't know about *love*."

The way she said it made involuntary tears spring to Genevieve's eyes. She turned back to the piano, actually seeing the printed pages of music in her head. She could play it from memory. It wasn't just *muscles* that remembered.

"I haven't played this for some time," she murmured.

"You won't fail." The way Trevelyan said it gave her all the confidence she needed.

Genevieve played *Widmung* as she had never played it before. She had learned all about passion right here on Djangala. The man she had found it with was seated only a short space away from her. Caught up in the moment, she felt Catherine's passionate love and her dire fate retreat to the back of her mind.

Trevelyan was due to pick her up in ten minutes. They weren't taking the horses, but the Jeep. Genevieve was trying to sort through her feelings. She had to consider he now knew *exactly* who she was—a bestselling author. It was obvious Liane had made it her business to ferret out her pen-name, probably finding out quite a bit about her and her family in the process. But mercifully there would be no apparent connection to Catherine.

Once more the familiar white-hot rush of excitement the minute she saw him. He stepped out of the Jeep, a tall, striking figure, his akubra pulled down at a rakish angle on his tanned forehead. There were no words she could come up with even as an author to describe his effect on her. *Mesmerising* didn't say it. She was a woman in thrall, confronting the reality that she was hopelessly, helplessly in love with him. Indeed, under his sway.

But was there a huge distinction between being *in* love and knowing oneself loved? The line for her was becoming more and more blurred. In a way, she almost wanted her old self back. The cool, composed and successful Genevieve, who had been gaining control of her life. The Genevieve she was now was no match for Trevelyan. Her feelings for him were pushing her to the very limits.

She rushed to meet him, not wanting to keep him waiting. He was staring right at her. No smile. She didn't smile either. She saw he had made an instant check on her: protective sunglasses, hat, etc. She had brought her own straw hat instead of the akubra she had been presented with. Her straw hat was more feminine, and it fitted her head better.

"All right. Let's get going." His long shadow fell over her.

She wasted no time, throwing her hat into the back before climbing into the passenger seat. It had been a day of blazing heat. It was getting towards late afternoon now, and the air had cooled, but chances were they would have a thunderstorm. The Dry was moving towards the tropical Wet. A storm had threatened the afternoon before—a spectacular display, but as frequently happened coming to nothing. From long years of drought followed by two years of unprecedented torrential rain people on the land had become wary of gathering storms. Often they brought flash floods—the cause of the death of city girl Sondra Wakefield.

Inside the Jeep the very air was trembling. Genevieve averted her head, looking fixedly out the window at the flying miles. In the heat the silvery-blue fire of mirage was abroad. It created so many quivering illusions, or really *delusions*, she could see how lost explorers had been tricked into believing glassy lakes of water weren't all that far off if only they could survive to reach them. Fascinating, but cruel.

Genevieve looked up at the sky. The contrast between the cloudless peacock-blue and what was happening on the horizon was extraordinary. Piles upon piles of incandescent cumulus clouds were massing: purple, dark grey, streaks of livid green surely denoting electrical charges, streaks of crimson, a rolling line of navy blue nearest the horizon. That could only mean a fierce electrical storm was threatening, although here and there the anvil-shaped masses were shot through by glittering swords of sunlight.

There was a purple haze over the jagged line of ridges where they were heading. The Hill Country guarded the galleries of aboriginal art on the station. She had seen over the years many wonderful non-sacred paintings on canvas and on bark. Aboriginal art had established itself in major art galleries all over the world, despite the fact it was such a departure from Western modernism, or maybe because of it.

As they drove across the vast trackless wilderness she was amazed by the thick vivid green herbage that was strewn across the Spinifex country: bright bursts of pink, yellow and cobalt blue wildflowers were scattered all over in huge patches. Flights of budgerigar zoomed ahead of them in their unique squadron formation. To Genevieve's fascinated eyes they looked like long flowing bolts of emerald silk tipped with gold. It was a sight she had come to treasure. The bauhinias—the beautiful orchid trees that only a couple of weeks before she had so admired, bright with pink, white, cerise or purple blossom—were stripped of their seasonal glory. The spent petals had dropped in masses, like snow in the desert.

About half a mile from their destination she dared to glance across at Trevelyan's handsome profile. It could have adorned a coin, she thought. She was anxious to know what was ahead of her. For a moment she thought he was about to speak, but apparently he thought better of it.

"So what's wrong?" She was so nervous she jumped in—just to get it over.

"Did I say something was wrong?" he countered, without turning to her.

"You don't have to. It's written all over you."

"Who can escape your percipience?" he said suavely.

That stung. "It saved Kit," she reminded him.

He did glance at her then. "So it did. I'm sorry."

"Apology accepted. You're a man who wouldn't apologise often." She turned her head again to look out of the window. It was a gesture of refuge.

"That's good, coming from you." Mockery laced his voice.

They might have been cocooned inside a bubble. Excitement was building—dark and disturbing. "So what has Liane been up to?"

"Funny you should ask that."

Genevieve shrugged. "She's obviously done some checking on me. I knew she would. Your ex-fiancée is clinging to the belief the two of you are going to get back together again."

"And *you* say we won't?" He flashed her a satirical look.

"No, you won't," she said quietly. "Liane did something you considered unforgivable. No coming back from there. I understand perfectly. My ex-fiancé betrayed me with my own stepsister."

All was silent. "Good God!" he breathed. "Betrayal on two fronts."

"I don't think I can ever forgive her," Genevieve said, eyes cast down. "It took me most of my life to realise Carrie-Anne had problems with me. I'm a few years older. You know all about sibling rivalry—though she wasn't a true sibling, but my stepmother's daughter. From the beginning Carrie-Anne had to have what I had. I suppose you could say in a weird way she wanted to *be* me. Anyway, that's a chapter closed."

"What she did was very wrong." Trevelyan passed judgement. "One can only wonder at your nameless fiancé's blindness and stupidity."

She turned her head towards him. "I could say the same, perhaps, of Liane?"

He gave a brief laugh that held little humour. "At least we like *something* about one another. That admitted, I'm not sharing my secrets with you, Genevieve Grenville aka Michelle Laurent. You've forfeited my confidence by not sharing your secrets with me. So you're a bestselling author! Congratulations. I can't for the life of me think why you found it necessary to hide the fact."

"It *was* Liane, wasn't it?" she asked.

"You're the mind-reader. Of *course* it was Liane. She's fiercely jealous of you."

"And why would that be?" she asked, in a tightly controlled voice.

"Oh, please—it's not exactly one of life's unanswerable questions, is it? Women *know* these things. She knows I'm attracted to you."

"Despite having so many suspicions and doubts? Tell me—I'm curious."

"You have the nerve to ask?" He swung his head.

"Are we going to have a set-to?" She pushed distracted fingers into her hair, held at the nape by an antique gold clasp that had belonged to Michelle. She had long forsaken the offending bun.

"Set-to?" He laughed. "A bit old fashioned, isn't it?"

"All right—a blue. A ding-dong fight."

"What would be the point?"

She released a long breath. "I'm not going to miss you when I leave."

"Oh, yes, you are!" His black eyes glinted. "Besides, I haven't said you *can* leave. Not until we get to the bottom of *why* exactly you're here on—my—land." He spaced out the words for emphasis. "Anyway, that can wait. We're here."

Genevieve stared up at the ancient rust-red eroded ridges. Some pointed jagged fingers to the blue sky. The ridges weren't all that high, but the flatness of the plains country below exaggerated their height. Not far from where Trevelyan had parked the Jeep a mob of brumbies—a grey stallion, obviously the leader, two chestnuts with white blazes, and two liver bays—were standing up to their flat knees in the wildflowers that swam across the top of the tall grasses. Heads were turned alertly towards them.

Genevieve, the horse lover, paused to take in the picture they made, while Trevelyan paid no attention. This was an everyday sight to him.

"Put your hat on," he said.

"I was about to." Defiance spiked her voice. "I'm not a schoolgirl out on a day trip." No chance of being cool and unflappable with Trevelyan.

"Why would a red-head not have a temper?" He gave her mutinous face a look of languid amusement. Sunlight was falling through the weave of her straw hat, throwing little glittery chinks of light on her flawless skin. "I've told you the akubra offers more protection. But you don't listen. Turn the sides *down*, not up." He waited while she did. "Okay, let's see the main cave. Obviously we have to do a bit of climbing, but at least you're wearing the right boots."

At one point she made a little agitated sound, fearing she might lose her footing on the rubble, only his hand shot out to clasp hers.

The intoxicating feeling of skin on skin! Strange the way he had of not only commanding her thoughts, but her body's responses as well. Did anyone really understand powerful physical attraction? she pondered. She had two hearts. One was bouncing around in her chest. The other one had mounted into her throat. It was no easy thing to fall victim to overwhelming desire, and it offered no peace.

The sun was still shining brilliantly, but she could *smell* the storm. The active oxygen in the air, the ozone and its clean fresh scent. The scent was intensified by the sun's discharge both before and especially after a lightning storm. She knew in her bones *this* was the day the storm would break.

He kept tight hold of her hand as they moved along the face of a long-eroded escarpment. Genevieve was stepping very carefully. Small showers of pebbles dislodged by their footsteps were racing with a clatter down the slopes. A reckless wind had sprung up, coming from the north-east and hitting her face like a sharp smack. Trevelyan's akubra was withstanding the sudden wind change. She was forced to hold her straw hat in place. She snatched it off before it went sailing away.

They had passed several small openings that could be the homes of desert creatures, but Trevelyan kept them moving along the narrow crumbling track until they were outside the neck of a cave much higher and larger. The opening was a perfect oval.

"Stand here for a moment," he said, pointing to an exact spot against the red ochre rock wall. The man was well used to obedience. "I'll check inside."

At once she thought of snakes. Desert taipans. God! Dragon Lizards would be lovable pets by comparison.

A moment later Trevelyan, dipping his dark head so as not to knock it, signalled to her that it was okay to enter. Her head easily cleared the neck of the cave. Brilliant sunlight slanted steeply into the interior, but she knew that wasn't going to last. The burning ochres of the wild landscape, so beautiful in their savage way, were soon replaced by violet shadows. After the heat of the desert the interior of the cave was of infinite coolness. What a benediction! She threw her straw hat onto the clean sand. It landed right beside Trevelyan's cream akubra. Fascinated, she lifted her glowing head to the rock walls, worried the light might fail in the violence of a storm.

She felt just as she would if confronted by paintings in an art gallery. Only these were individual drawings, executed in an extremely lively manner. Even the high ceiling some eight feet high at the centre was covered.

"How did they get up there?" she asked in some wonderment.

He watched as a beam of reflected light caught her sumptuous hair. "They would have devised something. Not many people get to see this cave. One reason why the drawings are so well preserved."

"Then I'm privileged."

He nodded. "It's actually quite an important gallery. On the ceiling are the so-called floral designs. Various wild creatures, plenty of them mythical, are engraved on the back wall. The wall you're facing has hunting and ceremonial scenes. None of the rock engravings have anything to do with sorcery, considering sorcery was rife in this area. The totemic designs are considered to be extremely good. A year or two ago we had an emeritus professor from the University of Western Australia give us his opinion and offer conservation advice. As this gallery is on Djangala we have an obligation to preserve it."

"Of course," she murmured, continuing her tour. "That can't be a crocodile, surely?" She paused before an engraving. "And fish?"

"You're forgetting the inland sea of pre-history. Lake Eyre, right at the heart of the continent, has filled twice in the last two years. Unbelievable. I flew over it both times. It certainly brought to mind the Inland Sea."

A tremendous flash of lightning prevented any further comment, its blinding brilliance illuminating the interior of the cave like a stage set. Automatically Genevieve began to count off the seconds before they experienced what had to be a clap of thunder of Wagnerian proportions. It came right on cue reverberating so powerfully over the walls of the cave she had to put her hands to her ringing ears.

"It's going to pour, isn't it?" she asked Trevelyan.

Something was very delicately, very dangerously poised over them. The sword of Damocles? She thought a single movement could bring it down.

"But then you knew that."

"Of course I did. I've lived here all my life. You're quite safe here. The cave is deep. And you won't be able to get away. You and I are going to have a long overdue talk, Genevieve."

Tumult set itself up, echoing the tumult of the storm. "What do you imagine I'm going to tell you?"

"Why do you want to dig up the rubble of the past?" he asked in brusque interrogation.

"Why do you want to *hide* it?" she countered, thinking the wildness of the storm was enfolding them in great wings. Everything had the high definition of one of her dreams.

"Simple," he clipped out. "I don't want to cause my family grief. The pain of some old stories has never healed."

"*One* old story, don't you mean?" She issued the challenge as if she could no longer hold on to it. "Like the fate of the young blonde woman Hester loved? All that remains of her are memories and old photographs. Hester left it to you to tell me. But you're crying off, aren't you?

"Oh, spare me!" he exclaimed. "And what's all this nonsense about Hester *loving* the young woman?"

"Why don't you give her a name?" Genevieve looked right back at him.

"This is *personal*, isn't it?" His tone gripped like a vice.

"Personal?" Her voice rose.

"Yes, damn it! You aren't talking about someone in *my* family's past. You're not here gathering information, or inspiration for another bestseller. This is exactly what I say—personal." Anger was glittering in his eyes.

Genevieve shook her head, thinking everything was slipping out of her grasp. "You don't need to know any of that."

He could feel himself losing control. Only this woman could do it to him. The fact that he wanted her so badly even now only increased his anger. "*Don't* I? Who the hell do you think you are?" He moved closer.

She was taller than average, but he made her feel like a doll. "Well, I thought I was here in the capacity of ghostwriter." Instinctively she backed away.

He couldn't trust himself not to shake her. He could even feel his hand around the back of her neck. "Genevieve, I want answers, not evasions." He spoke with blunt force. "What a shock it must have been for you when that McGuire woman asked if you'd like a short stint in the Outback—moreover on a historic station. Just a bit of ghost-writing—a piece of cake! It must have seemed like a God-sent opportunity."

Genevieve found herself clutching at his arm. "What really happened to Catherine?"

He shook her off, afraid he would take what he so desperately wanted. "How did you know it was *Catherine*? Hester didn't put a name to the young woman in the photograph—which, incidentally, I've just seen for the *first* time."

He was staring at her as if she were the very image of someone from the past. Genevieve turned her head away, half blinded by another searing flash of lightning.

"Catherine Lytton is the key to everything, isn't she?" he said. "Otherwise you'd never have come here."

She didn't answer. Her nerves were terribly on edge. She thought if he touched her her mood could even turn hysterical.

"I'll take that as a yes. Imagine—we'd never have met!" he said with great irony. Her beauty—luminous, delicate—her desirability was breaking over him in dizzying waves.

Genevieve dared not meet his eyes. "Haven't you got *anything* to say, Bret?"

The lightning that flickered in the cave, lit one side of his striking face; the other was in a shadow. "I think I should know *your* story first," he said. "You have a family connection to Catherine Lytton?"

There was nothing she could do but tell the truth. "Yes, I do," she admitted, her voice splintered. "Sooner or later it was all going to come out. The big surprise is Liane didn't dig deeper. Catherine Lytton was my kinswoman—first cousin to my maternal grandmother."

He stared back at her with a frown. "And you've applied yourself to finding out more about her? She died in a tragic accident long before either of us was born. The accident was thoroughly investigated." There was a real harshness to his voice. "There were no witnesses. She must have stepped too close to the crumbling edge of the escarpment. You could see how easily sections of the rock face sheared off as we climbed up here. Everyone could understand what so easily happened."

She felt more secure now. She had proof. "Did everyone know Hester was in love with Catherine?"

He loomed over her, one of his hands executing a chopping, dismissive gesture. "Nonsense!"

"*Ask* her. She'll tell you." Genevieve clung to her belief. "It's not so unusual, is it? These out-of-the-mould love stories have been happening since the beginning of time."

"God, I can't wear this," he groaned. "Genevieve, you're just embellishing a good story."

"I'm not going to *write* it, Bret," she hastened to reassure him. "Nothing will go into the book if both of you consider it taboo."

"Here we go again! *Taboo*!" he exploded. "I think you've fallen victim to your own imagination. It is, after all, exceptionally vivid."

"It goes a lot deeper than that, Bret," she said, desperate for his help. "My grandmother had in her possession a letter from Catherine, saying she and your grandfather Geraint had fallen in love, but everyone thought he would marry Patricia. Patricia who became your grandmother *after* Catherine was killed."

His handsome mouth was set in a hard line. "Killed? For God's sake, Genevieve, what are you saying?"

She could see he was furious, horrified—both. "That's all I know." Though he was standing very still, she felt thoroughly intimidated. She loved this man. But if she'd had any hope with him she was fast losing it. "I wasn't told the story directly. It was by sheer chance I overheard a conversation between my grandparents years ago. My grandmother was extremely upset, weeping bitterly. All these years later I think it *wrong* to leave Catherine's death as a tragic accident. Someone must have been with her. Someone, moreover, who wanted to get rid of her."

He was appalled. Frustrated. He wanted to shake some sense into her. But most of all he wanted to pick her up in his arms, lay her down on the sandy floor of the cave, make far from gentle love to her. "That's *your* version, is it, Michelle Laurent, bestselling writer of psychological thrillers? My family knows the true version even if *your* family don't."

Her breath was coming in gasps. "How about you ask Hester? She's an old woman, yet she's still consumed by guilt, grief—who knows? There wasn't just an eternal triangle going on—Geraint, Patricia, Catherine. Hester came into it as well."

He moved with superb ease, backing her up against a smooth rock wall. "So you want *me* to look into it before someone pushes *you* off a cliff?"

Her green eyes searched his. "I trust you, Bret. You have power. Maybe that person was none of them but someone else?" Out of nowhere, she was rocked by doubt.

"Ah, Genevieve!" Trevelyan made a groaning sound deep in his throat. "This all sounds mad to me."

"But the story was hushed up, wasn't it?" she persisted. "In all the documents, photographs, information. Hester didn't mention one word about Catherine. It all came to a head when I saw the photograph. She wanted it kept hidden, but it was stuck to another photograph. You must have noticed the possessive way Hester's hand was clamped on Catherine's arm. Patricia, after all, was Catherine's friend, not Hester's. Did your father never speak of it?"

Outside the wind had dropped. The great torrents of rain were easing back. A blast of fresh fragrant air swept into the cave, but it couldn't cool the heated atmosphere within.

Trevelyan stood very still. "Not *one* word."

"Odd, don't you think?"

"Not at all odd." His tone was curt. "You didn't

know my father. He was a fine man, but a hard man. A real authoritarian. Anyone would tell you that. He was extremely tough on us all after our mother left."

"Maybe she found him too tough as well?"

Something smouldered in his dark eyes. "Let it go, Genevieve," he warned. "And don't stare at me with those great green eyes. My father didn't confide in any of his children. Certainly not to discuss an old tragedy. He would have considered it of no account."

"Even when it involved his mother and father? Catherine was Patricia's *friend*."

Provoked, he snatched hold of her shoulders. "A friend who betrayed Patricia behind her back?"

"They weren't engaged." She flew to Catherine's defence.

"They would have been. Look, I don't want to hear about this again, Genevieve. What good will it do, raking up the past?"

She held his dark gaze, unmoved. "Catherine won't let it rest."

His dynamic features were drawn so taut it threw into high relief his strongly modelled bone structure. "Please, I don't need any of the paranormal stuff. Catherine Lytton is dead. All three of them are dead. My grandparents *and* your Catherine. You're working yourself up for nothing."

"I want to know."

He did shake her then. "When it will stay a secret for all eternity? All of them are *gone*, Genevieve. You want someone to pay? Is that it?"

She had a sensation of swaying. He gathered her up against his chest. "I'm sure they *have* paid, Bret." She looked up at him. "Guilt is torture. I just want to *know*—don't you see? Catherine deserves it."

His stare held ironic reproof. "You're obviously one of those people who can't leave things alone."

"I must be," she whispered. "You talked about fate, Bret. Fate brought me here."

He had to listen to that. "So fate decided to seek you out?"

"Choose what you want to believe."

"It's not a question of what I *want* to believe," he returned angrily, suddenly realising the amount of pressure he must be putting on her delicate shoulders. Instantly his grip lightened. "Am I free to choose *you*?" He reached out a hand to unfasten the gold clasp in her hair. "What means the most to you, then? The connection we've had from the very beginning? Or are you dead set on juggling random pieces to fit your puzzle? Seems to me it's more important to you to prove there was more to Catherine Lytton's death than what was confirmed."

She was almost in tears, so powerfully was she aroused. "It won't let me *be*, Bret. I didn't ask for any of this. I know I could be destroying what it is we have. But none of you has forgotten the old story. Hester to this day is downright tormented."

He too was unnerved by her intensity. "So you think Hester can solve the mystery? What is it you want her to say? *She* pushed Catherine over the cliff in a jealous rage? Is that what you want? As far as I'm concerned this whole damned thing is over the top."

She shook her head violently. Such a clamour was within her. "I only want the truth."

"*This* is the truth." His tall, powerful body radiated a high level of sexual tension. "The here and now. Not some old tragic story. Life *is* chaos. Things just happen. We don't do the directing. You would never have come here if the opportunity hadn't fallen into your lap."

"Fate, not chaos," she maintained.

"Okay, okay." He was trying to get a grip on his turbulent emotions. "You're entitled to your opinion. But I find it unacceptable to cast doubts on *my* people. Hester might be a throwback to an earlier century, but I'm convinced she would never deliberately cause anyone harm."

Her breath stabbed. "So this is a witch hunt?"

"You have to admit what's going on here is very strange. I'm just an ordinary guy, Genevieve."

"Ordinary?" She had to laugh at that. "How can you describe yourself as ordinary? You're Master of Djangala and God knows what else. Try telling the ordinary man or woman in the street *you're* ordinary."

He truly believed his nerves would snap. His body was flooded with fierce desire and he had to listen to *this*. "Stop it, Genevieve, for God's sake. I really can't talk about it. Not now."

"Please, Bret. Bear with me. In my dream—the dream about Sondra—Catherine was with her. They were arm-in-arm, like friends."

It was inconceivable to take a woman against her will, but her nearness and the accusations she was making were tearing him up. He couldn't think about anything else but her. He was human. He was a man alone with the woman he fiercely wanted. "Genevieve, I'm finding this unbearable," he said tautly. "I only want to make love to you."

The expression in his eyes shook her to the core. "I *want* you to make love to me." It was such a release to just say it.

"Then *stop.* I beg you." Hardly knowing what he was doing, his hunger was so great, he began to kiss her—her temples, her cheeks, her long satiny throat—pressing his mouth against the pulsing blue artery. She was quite extraordinary. He knew that, and he loved her for it. At the same time her "gift" was creating an intolerable space between them. He couldn't allow it. He intended to have her. He intended marriage. He intended she be the mother of his children. He pressed her beautiful yielding body to him, desperate to possess it.

"I know I seem strange to you," she murmured.

"Strange? God, Genevieve, you have me in thrall."

Was there the faintest nuance of sexual hostility in his voice? Adam tempted by Eve? Man forever tempted by woman? "You don't like it?"

"I *love* it," he groaned. "In *some* ways."

"You're wary of the things you can't understand?"

"You said it." He tipped up her chin, the better to move his caressing mouth beneath it. Her body had grown languorous with desire. She was half slumped in his arms. He could fell her heartbeat against the palm that cupped her breast. The womanly fragrance of her was a powerful intoxicant.

"I think someone attacked Catherine," Genevieve said, unable to stop herself even now. "That's what she's trying to tell me."

It wrung his heart and aroused a deep ache. He wanted to know every last little thing about her? Well, this was part of her. In some way he thought she was being controlled. He would have to contend with that, even if he didn't understand it.

"So you believe that justifies your subterfuge?"

The air was cracking with instability. What was truly extraordinary was that although they were in some ways in conflict the physical desire they felt for each other carried on unabated. The mind, the reasoning power, had little control over the demands their bodies were making. It was profoundly erotic, this desire to know one another in every possible way.

Genevieve's whole body was shaking with pleasure. She had never known herself capable of such intense reactions. "You changed me," she said.

He stared into her eyes. "*Did* I?"

"You know you did." In the scintillating warmth

inside the cave she began very slowly to unbutton his soft denim shirt with trembling fingers, all the while staring up into his handsome tautened face.

She could bring such music to her voice, he thought, a man seized by a spell. There had been little joy in his family life. Not since their mother had run off. Derryl was having a job trying to sort himself out. Romayne at least had found her soul mate. The Trevelyans had always had wealth, not happiness. As his father's heir, he'd had plenty of hard work, plenty of self-denial, big responsibilities. He could throw it all over. He had more than enough money to last him for ever, but to quit was unthinkable. He had a job to do, but he wanted the right woman by his side.

That woman was Genevieve, hell-bent on unravelling a mystery.

His shirt was hanging loose, exposing his superb physique. Genevieve put her hands on his body, moving her hand in little caressing semi-circles over his darkly bronzed skin, splaying her fingers, running them down to the waistband of his jeans. His body was marvellous to her, but she knew she could get burned.

"Where are we going with this, Genevieve?" Trevelyan spoke with hard urgency. "Talk to me.

Look at me. You can't do this to me and then think you can call a halt."

Flames were fanning out through her body. "Why are you letting an old story come between us? You weren't part of it. What have you to fear?"

He caught her roving hands, holding them fast. "The only thing I fear is you. Crazy isn't it? For me to fear a slip of a woman."

"Would it matter if I said I loved you?"

He took such a deep breath his chest heaved. "*Do* you?" There was pain in every part of his body. And she was the cause of it.

"For the first time in my life," she murmured.

He forced her fiery head up. "Are you trying to melt my hard heart?"

"I am," she whispered, her green gaze intent on him. "You're here. I'm here. We're together. I *want* you to make love to me."

Her voice, though soft as a whisper, seemed to echo eerily through the cave. It was as if those very words had been uttered by a young woman a long time ago.

"You don't fear being compromised? I have no protection. I didn't bring you here to have sex. It's as I've told you, Genevieve. I have a responsibility towards you."

"I know." Only she stepped right into his arms, putting her mouth to his naked chest, unashamed. Overwhelmed by the moment she locked her arms around his lean waist. Her hair slid forward, muffling her words. "It's a safe time for me. I have never, *ever* asked a man to make love to me."

"Not the man you were engaged to?" His gaze burned over her.

She looked up at him with those large almond-shaped green eyes. "It was always a case of the other way around. I couldn't have been in love with him. This proves it, doesn't it? I never felt remotely what I feel for you. I was a different person then. I might have lived in another galaxy."

"Well, you're in *my* world now," he said, with rough emphasis. "This could go very wrong as well as very right, Genevieve."

The hectic flush in her cheeks had suffused her whole body. "I don't care." She had stopped thinking. She was totally focused on getting what she so wanted.

"Strangely enough, neither do I."

Desire was roaring through him like a storm. He wanted above anything to be inside her. One day in the not distant future she would give birth to their child. Their first child, hopefully. He wanted a daughter who looked just like her mother. He had thought from time to time he might be condemned to a hard existence, full of responsibility and a certain isolation. His beautiful Genevieve had changed all that.

His joy was immense.

CHAPTER NINE

THE western sky was aflame before Trevelyan found his way down from the escarpment where Catherine Lytton had fallen all those years ago. Boughs whipped around him as he made his descent from the eroded plateau to where he had parked the Jeep, nosed into the shade of some acacias. He had to see what he could do for Genevieve—the woman he loved. He had to put her mind at rest.

Their coming together in the rock cave had been pure magic. Love *was* magic. Sacred in some way. The memory of those glorious stolen hours remained. Nothing had ever felt like that—the tremendous build-up of *need* that was agony, and then the tremendous release.

She had taken him deep into her body, and into the chambers of her heart. He had to do something for her now. He would speak to Hester. Try to get her to remember. Until he did, he and Genevieve were in a sort of limbo.

He had found it incredible to hear Catherine had written to her cousin of a love bond that had grown between his grandfather and her. Could it be true? Hester would surely know.

Something had broken Hester. Back from England on holiday long ago, she had never returned to take up her promising career.

Hester and her brother, Geraint, had been very close. It was true she had adored him. But what of Catherine of the long blonde hair and radiant blue eyes? *Had* Hester fallen in love with Patricia's friend, hardly realising what was happening to her? To love another woman... She would have known that would never have been accepted within the family.

But Genevieve's instincts were what directed her. Instincts and dreams. She wanted to shine a light on the past. He felt compelled to help.

Hester had heard his loud rap on her door. "It's me, Hester," Trevelyan called. "May I come in?"

Hester padded to the door, clutching her chest. She had always known this day would come. She couldn't go on enduring the pain. The memory of Catherine's last day on earth came back to her. Catherine had been totally innocent of her feelings for her. But, oh, the ache of loneliness, of wanting to take Catherine in her arms, tell her how much she meant to her.

She'd had little affection in her life from her mother. Her father and her brother had loved her and been proud of her. Hester had always thought her mother felt only relief when she had gone away to further her studies in London. She had no idea where all the warmth had gone.

Catherine, her beauty and the sunniness of her nature had swept all before her. Catherine had been a beautiful person. A child of light.

To Hester's shock, Bret was accompanied by Genevieve. "What is *she* doing here?" Her eyes shifted almost frantically from one to the other.

"Forgive me, Ms Trevelyan, but Bret wanted me here," Genevieve intervened. She hadn't wanted to come, but Bret had insisted. She had started it, after all, but she had no wish to see this fierce, rather terrible old lady disintegrate under questioning.

As it was, Hester fell back in apparent shock. "What *is* this?"

"Something that can't wait any longer, Hester." Bret moved past her into the room, with Genevieve a faltering pace behind. "The last thing we want is to distress you, but the subject of Catherine Lytton—you remember her?—has come up."

Hester responded with a look of utter amazement. "How? Why? An old tragic accident," she snapped.

"If you could just tell us what you know," Bret answered, quietly enough but with a bite to it. "May we sit down?"

Hester flapped her hands, taking the most ornate chair herself. "The verdict of accidental death was accepted. Why bring up such a painful episode now?"

"Actually, Hester, you were the one who brought it to mind with that photograph. You were in it. You had your hand on Catherine Lytton's shoulder."

"So?" Hester retorted, as if she had no need to answer anyone's questions.

Bret and Genevieve exchanged glances. "You loved her, Hester?" Genevieve prompted, very gently.

Bret spread his hands "We make no judgements, Hester. Love is love, wherever we find it. All we want is for you to tell us what you can of her last day. We realise it's very painful for you, but it might help to make the bad memories go away."

"We? *We?*" Hester's dark eyes burned like coals. "You care for this young woman, Bret?" she asked sharply.

"I do," Bret said, reaching across to take Genevieve's hand.

"Dear God!" Hester sat in her outdated splendour, hands clasped tight, her stringy throat working.

"Is it possible you were with Catherine at the end?" Genevieve asked. "She stepped too close to the edge and fell?"

Hester put shaking arthritic hands over her face. "I might have been able to save her had I been there," she said harshly. "She was alone. I was where I said I was. No one has ever doubted me."

"Only there are some doubts now," Bret said. "It seems to me no one was all that sure where the others were—except my grandmother, who was with the housekeeper at the time. This is a big house, after all. Someone could have been out with Catherine?"

Hester waved a hand aloft. "I had a friend from London staying with us at the time. A brilliant young violinist—Adeline Baker. Like me, she didn't fulfil her promise," she snorted.

"Is she still alive?" Trevelyan asked.

"She could be." Hester looked as though she couldn't care less. "At that time we were best friends. We made music together. We had so much in common. We went everywhere together in London. I was often invited to her family's country home. And I was fool enough once to confide in Addie the emotions I felt for Catherine."

Bret started to feel hollow inside. It was coming—the telling disclosure. "And?"

Hester fired up. "And Adeline was *disgusted*. I'll never forget how she turned on me. She wanted to leave, but she couldn't just up and go. She had to wait for transport."

"She was where at the time of Catherine's accident?" Trevelyan kept his eyes trained on his great-aunt's face.

"Somewhere around," Hester offered vaguely. "She had taken so violently against me. She made me feel like a really bad person. It can't be bad to love someone, can it?" She turned her head to appeal to Genevieve. "Nothing ever happened between Catherine and me."

Genevieve seized her moment. "What about between Catherine and your brother, who was expected to marry Patricia?"

Hester licked a salty tear off her upper lip. Genevieve got up quietly to find tissues.

"I could see Geraint was as captivated as I was," she said bleakly. "Patricia didn't stand a chance against Catherine."

"So you're saying he fell in love with Catherine too?" Bret now had confirmation of Genevieve's claim.

Grief came into Hester's sunken eyes. She grasped the tissue Genevieve had handed her from a box, used it to blow her nose. "Poor Geraint. Poor me. I can't talk about this any more, Bret. I know nothing else."

Genevieve knew intuitively Hester was lying.

Bret had no intention of letting Hester go either. "Where was Adeline Baker that day? You *do* know."

Hester began fiddling with the gold tassel on her robe. "Out riding. She was an excellent horse-woman."

"That's the tall young woman looking away in the photograph?" Trevelyan asked.

Hester was starting to look rattled. "Yes, that's

Addie. She let me know exactly how she felt. She *hated* Catherine. She thought Catherine was leading me on. Or it seemed that way to her. It was totally untrue." Hester couldn't stop her voice from trembling.

Trevelyan was getting a clearer picture. "So Catherine had gone riding; so had Adeline. It's quite possible Adeline went after her, seeking a confrontation?"

The more he probed, the more agitated Hester became. "Why are you doing this, Bret?"

"I *have* to. Catherine, you see, was Genevieve's maternal grandmother's first cousin. They were very close. Catherine wrote to her."

Hester's response surprised both Trevelyan and Genevieve. "I *knew* she wasn't who she said she was," she said wrathfully. "I used to catch glimpses of Catherine in her face and manner. I thought I was going ga-ga."

"Not you, Hester," Trevelyan said very dryly. "I think Adeline Baker and her whereabouts on that day should have been taken much more seriously."

"But she barely knew Catherine." Hester decided to offered a feeble protest. "She was a young woman of good family. No one wanted to draw Addie into it."

"So why all these years later would you have us believe Adeline *did* have something to do with it?" Trevelyan held Hester's eyes.

Hester shook her white head. "Addie would never have gone to such lengths."

"The two of you were to have returned to London together?" Genevieve asked, knowing they weren't getting the full truth.

Hester didn't deign to look at her. "Not possible," she said shortly.

"Only it *is* possible," Bret cut in. "Adeline could have gone after Catherine. She could have followed her to the escarpment."

"Which hardly makes her guilty of pushing Catherine off the cliff!" Hester hit back haughtily.

Trevelyan's mind was leaping from detail to detail, filling in the blanks. The irony was Adeline Baker might have harboured deep unresolved feelings for Hester. Hester had been a beautiful, gifted young woman.

"You didn't keep in touch with Adeline?" he asked.

Hester bridled. "The day she left she told me she never wanted to have anything to do with me again. No one has to tell me twice. I should never have told her of my feelings for Catherine."

"It's possible Adeline had feelings for *you*," Genevieve suggested. "Love, hate—different sides of the same coin."

A light in Hester's dark eyes flickered, then went out. "So Catherine won't go peacefully?"

"It seems not," Trevelyan said. "Genevieve believes in some strange way Catherine is haunting her."

"God knows she's haunted *me* all these years." Hester dredged up a jagged sigh. "But what proof is there of what really happened?"

"Adeline Baker may still be alive?"

"Bret, she'd be an old woman—like me." Hester shrugged that off.

"And could we really ruin what's left of her life?" Genevieve asked no one in particular, certain, without understanding why, that Adeline had done no wrong.

"If she took Catherine's?" Trevelyan challenged bluntly.

Hester lifted a heavily beringed hand. "Bret, I won't go on with this. I wouldn't have harmed a hair of Catherine's head. I loved her. The only person I've ever loved outside you, my father and my brother. I was never close to my mother. Even Derryl and Romayne seem like little strangers to me. My fault. I became a different person. Not a nice one. Losing Catherine finished me off. I'm innocent of any wrongdoing, but in my heart I've always felt I was to blame. Catherine has always been watching me. I can understand Genevieve's wanting to know. But I can offer you no more because I *know* no more."

"But you withheld from the investigation Adeline Baker's dislike of Catherine," Trevelyan couldn't prevent himself from saying.

Hester clasped her twisted, swollen fingers. "I wanted to say something. I was out of my mind with grief and worry. But I was a coward. If I'd pointed a finger at Addie, she would have spoken out against me. Turned my family against me. I had to measure the terrible reality of Catherine's death with what Adeline could do to me in retaliation. I kept quiet. I've paid for it ever since."

It was impossible to miss the deep well of emotion that flooded Hester's voice.

"What you're saying is your friend Adeline had far more to answer for than you?" Trevelyan asked. Hester was looking very old and defenceless. It upset him. His great-aunt had always been such a strange woman, but she was *family*.

"It was a cover-up in a way," Hester confessed

abruptly. "We all knew Geraint was fascinated by Catherine. He couldn't hide it. Certainly not from me or Patricia. But Patricia wouldn't have hurt a fly. If Addie *did* meet up with Catherine and confront her anything could have happened. Perhaps Catherine backed up dangerously close to the lip of the cliff? She should have been warned. If it *was* Addie with her, she got away with it. And I let her."

Trevelyan rose, looking down at his great-aunt from his lean height. "I'll check on your old friend Adeline Baker. I'll have it done quietly."

"She'll be dead." Hester looked desperate for it to be so.

"If she was involved, she will have been carrying an intolerable burden all these years." Like you, he thought.

Hester's eyes looked like the eyes of a condemned woman. "I should have spoken up long, long ago. Don't you see, Bretton? Catherine directed Genevieve here. Irrational, maybe, but what other explanation can there be? Coincidence? Catherine has never left." She shot a piercing look at Genevieve. "The book can't go ahead, of course. Out of the question. Genevieve knows too much. She can only be a reminder of Catherine. I want her to go away. My life has always been *meaning-less*. You were only indulging me, anyway, Bret. Genevieve must go. I would be doing you a big favour."

Trevelyan felt a rush of anger. "There's no question of Genevieve's going, Hester," he said, bringing to bear the full force of his authority.

Hester stared up at him. "You'd betray me? *You*?" she cried with renewed vigour. "It was the same with Geraint. You're crazy about her, aren't you?"

"Why all the drama?" He gave her a straight look. "Scarcely *crazy*, Hester. I *love* Genevieve. I want her for my wife. What we have is absolutely substantial. I recognised the woman I love the moment I laid eyes on her. You know all about the *coup de foudre*?"

Hester didn't look up. "What will happen will happen. I'll have no part of it."

In the hallway hung with beautiful paintings in gilded frames, Trevelyan looked at Genevieve. "Did you believe her?"

Genevieve met his searching gaze. "No."

Over dinner Derryl had his usual battery of complaints, but Trevelyan stopped him in mid-flow.

"The place for you, Derryl, would be the city of your choice. You've never cared for our way of life."

"I'm like my mother there," Derryl said, hunching his shoulders.

"You could probably visit her." Trevelyan chose that moment to drop his bombshell.

"Wh-a-a-t?" Derryl looked as stunned as if his brother had given him permission to drop in on the Queen of England.

"Life really is stranger than fiction," Trevelyan said. "It's only very recently, when I was going through Dad's papers, I've discovered a thick wad of letters he'd shoved well away. Letters our mother had sent us. Strangely Dad kept them— but he certainly didn't hand them over to *us*. We were brainwashed into believing our mother ran off with her lover. That's what Dad *wanted* us to believe. Poor old George Melville was the fall guy. Dad would never have allowed it, had it been true. George wouldn't have got off Djangala alive. There was no illicit love affair—just a long-standing friendship."

Derryl was hanging on his brother's every word. "You're serious?"

"I'd like *you* to be serious too," Trevelyan said firmly.

"God!" Derryl breathed, as if he was scarcely able to take in this revelation. "Do you intend to contact her?"

"Let's say I'm working towards it." Trevelyan turned his dark gaze to Genevieve. He had already confided in her. It was she who had convinced him he would always regret it if he didn't contact his mother. Better yet, invite her back to Djangala.

"Can I read her letters?" Derryl begged, looking immensely vulnerable.

"Of course you can," Trevelyan assured him. "Romayne will get hers as well. Dad hammered home the fact our mother had deserted him and us—her children. She had turned her back on her clear duty. The fact is we didn't so much lose our mother as she lost us. She had to pay for not remaining under Dad's total sway. That was what he wanted of all of us, wasn't it? He was *the boss*. Undoubtedly our mother had her reasons for leaving," he added grimly.

Derryl sprang up like a jack-in-the-box. "I can't wait to read them."

Trevelyan looked up at his brother. "You'll find

all the letters addressed to you on the desk in Dad's study."

"This is like a great clarion call!" Derryl whooped.

Genevieve and Trevelyan watched with great satisfaction as Derryl tore off in the direction of their late father's study.

They went for a walk in the garden. The night was blessedly cool after the heat of the day. Genevieve's long loose hair blew in the breeze that came in from the desert. A billion desert stars glittered in the velvety black backdrop of the sky. No need to look for the Southern Cross: it hung above them, so bright it seemed to draw them upwards.

"So what now?" Genevieve asked.

Trevelyan had an arm loosely around her waist. Now he pulled her closer. He could feel the tension in her body. He knew they would never get to the bottom of the mystery surrounding Catherine Lytton's death. He couldn't protect Genevieve from Hester's revelations, much as he wanted to.

"We can only go forward," he said. "Let this whole sorry business drop."

"It's certainly what Hester wants." Genevieve's

mind was in a spin. "I thought she was trying to lay the blame at Adeline's door."

"Who knows with Hester?" Trevelyan's answer was grim. "The whole thing is plausible only if Adeline had strong feelings for Hester—feelings that couldn't be brought out into the open. The young Hester would have had a lot to fear if her friend gave her sexual orientation away. Hester swears she had nothing to do with Catherine's tragic end, but she managed to let slip that *Adeline* hated Catherine, leaving us to believe that could have triggered a confrontation."

Genevieve flinched. "Does the story never stop changing? Hester has never mentioned a *thing* about Adeline Baker before. She flew under the radar."

"Maybe Adeline had her suspicions of Hester?" Trevelyan suggested.

"Doors open. Doors slam in your face," Genevieve said with deep regret.

"It's such a long time ago. Many of the people who figured in the story are long dead. I just saw a mystery that needed to be solved."

He turned her to face him. "Genevieve, you *must* consider for your own peace of mind there *was* no mystery. Just a terrible accident."

"Hester implied otherwise. You know she did," Genevieve said in a doleful voice.

"Hester's a great one for drama, but she's right about the family falling about in shock. Those were different days, Genevieve. Love between two women would have been seen as incredibly taboo."

"It's *wrong* to sit in judgement," Genevieve said. "Hester has as good as told us the great burden of guilt she bore was not because of anything she *did*, but rather what she *didn't* do."

"That's about it," Trevelyan said, with a finality that jolted Genevieve's heart. "I can only tell you with certainty what *I* feel. All I know, all I *can* know, all I care about is *you*, Genevieve. It grieves me this whole business is preying on your mind."

"Of course it is!" she cried. Her heat was beating madly. "It won't leave me, Bret. Please try to understand. I don't control these feelings. *Could* Adeline Baker still be alive?"

He tried as hard as he knew how to keep calm. "We can find out. People are living much longer these days through medical science."

"If she is alive, I'll get on a plane," Genevieve vowed.

"And do what?" Trevelyan asked, in a way that

made it sound foolish. "Go to her home? Attempt to interrogate her? That's if you're let in. More likely she'll call the police. Think about it, Genevieve. There's no satisfactory outcome to this. Adeline Baker wouldn't admit to anything even if she did consent to see you. Why should she? You would be raking over a very painful episode in her life. One she would want to forget. She and Hester were close friends, yet they've had no contact in all these long years."

"It wasn't an accident, Bret." Genevieve shook her head sadly. "It just did *not* happen the way everyone said."

Trevelyan agreed, in spite of himself. But he said nothing. He just held her. Catherine Lytton's story had taken on a life of its own.

"And what's to happen to me?" She lifted her face to him in distress. "I didn't even *know* you, Bret, but I fell in love with you. I didn't intend it. You didn't intend it. It's almost like the past reached out to bring us together."

"So think about that," he urged strongly. "How would either of us know if that wasn't Catherine's intention all along?"

Genevieve was startled. "I'd ask her if I could. Only the dead don't speak. They come to you in dreams. They walk towards you or they walk away from you. We can only dimly understand. Even before I arrived on Djangala I felt this sense of destiny. I was meant to meet you. You were meant to meet me. My mind and my body carry the conviction like the seed of truth. Hester won't want me here any longer, will she?"

A groan came from deep in Trevelyan's throat. "Hester has *no* say. None at all. I've done everything I can to look after her. It hasn't been easy. I've often felt Hester has a darkness inside her. I'm pretty sure my father felt the same way. But she is a woman of our family, and well up in years."

"She has money?"

"A lot," Trevelyan said, his handsome mouth compressed.

"She could have made a life of her own. Instead of that she let it all go—her career…"

"She couldn't move away. She must have felt there was nothing left for her if she did. God, Genevieve, I don't want to talk about Hester any more. She's another responsibility I have to carry. I want to talk about *us*." Passionately he took her face between his hands, bending his head low so he could press his hungry mouth against hers.

"Hester has *no* say, Genevieve," he repeated emphatically.

"But she *doesn't* want me around."

He drew her into his close embrace. "I won't allow Hester to cast a shadow over us, Genevieve. You've changed my life. Even if you went away I could never forget you. But that's not going to happen. You have *me* to hold on to now. We have a life before us, full of wonderful things as long as we're together. You believe that, don't you? Tell me you do?"

She turned up her face. "I love you, Bret. I love you with every breath I take, with every beat of my heart. It's a tremendous thing to love someone that much. I am greatly blessed."

Trevelyan felt jubilant, yet immensely humbled. "Then I need your promise you'll marry me—and *soon*," he said sweepingly. "There's not a single atom of me that could bear to let you go. I want your promise you will never leave me."

"Leave you?" she echoed, hot blood rushing to every extremity. "When you bring me closer and closer to fulfilment and joy? When a heart is truly given it can *never* be withdrawn."

Here at last. Here at last! He was swept by

elation. *The woman I love. The woman I want to share my life with.*

"You have to be with me tonight." Genevieve— his woman—so passionate, so loving, so open to him.

"Oh, yes," she whispered.

"Let's go inside now. I know other things matter, my love, but nothing matters more to me than *you.*"

And that was the way it was to remain for ever.

EPILOGUE

THE passing of Ms Hester Trevelyan of historic Djangala Station in the Brisbane hospital to which she had been airlifted was treated with professional respect by the media. Ms Trevelyan, after all, had been a member of a prominent and distinguished Outback family—a true pastoral dynasty.

No one knew how many private tears were shed. The Trevelyans were very private people. And as was nearly always the case, Hester Trevelyan's sins were buried with her.

Much was made of the fact she had been denied by only a week or two the great pleasure of seeing her great-nephew Bretton Trevelyan, present Master of Djangala Station, married to the beautiful Genevieve Grenville, who just happened to be Michelle Laurent, the bestselling author. The wedding had not been the marvellous society spectacle women's magazines had been hoping for. It had been a private ceremony on the historic station with only friends and family, including the bridegroom's mother, who it was thought had been estranged from the family for some years. Apparently that was no longer the case.

The first leg of their honeymoon was reported as being in Hong Kong, and from there the great cities of Europe, taking in New York and San Francisco on the way back to Australia.

"What are you thinking, my love?" Genevieve, dressed in a sheer white nightgown trimmed with silver, came behind her husband, laying her radiant head against his broad back.

"What a sight!" he said, drawing her hands around him. They were looking down at Central Park through a window of their suite in one of New York's most prestigious hotels. "It's been the most wonderful honeymoon any man and woman could possibly dream of—"

"But she wants to go home," she broke in, giving a low laugh.

"You too?" He swung to face her.

"Me too," she said, with a richly contented smile. "My love for Djangala is scarcely less than my wonderful husband's!"

"That means so much to me!" Trevelyan heard his own grateful sigh. "It will be waiting for us, Genevieve. Welcoming us."

On a wave of jubilation he scooped his beautiful wife up into his arms, carrying her back to bed.

He bent over her, his brilliant dark eyes aflame. "I adore you. You know that?"

"I *should*." Genevieve had never felt so womanly, so wondrously desirable in her life. She stretched luxuriously, before reaching up to lock her arms around her husband's neck. "Come to bed," she whispered, letting her head fall back and closing her eyes.

This was Catherine's true legacy, she thought, her heart at peace. Whatever she had been looking for, she had found it. Catherine had brought into her life her husband, her passionate lover, her dearest and best friend.

And Bret, loving his wife so much, had determined he would never tell her that as Hester had been being wheeled into the operating theatre for what should have been a minor operation she had looked up at him, her formidable old face etched with anguish.

"It was never Addie," she said.

* * * * *

Mills & Boon® Large Print

May 2012

THE MAN WHO RISKED IT ALL
Michelle Reid

THE SHEIKH'S UNDOING
Sharon Kendrick

THE END OF HER INNOCENCE
Sara Craven

THE TALK OF HOLLYWOOD
Carole Mortimer

MASTER OF THE OUTBACK
Margaret Way

THEIR MIRACLE TWINS
Nikki Logan

RUNAWAY BRIDE
Barbara Hannay

WE'LL ALWAYS HAVE PARIS
Jessica Hart

0412 Rom LP

Mills & Boon® Large Print

June 2012

AN OFFER SHE CAN'T REFUSE
Emma Darcy

AN INDECENT PROPOSITION
Carol Marinelli

A NIGHT OF LIVING DANGEROUSLY
Jennie Lucas

A DEVILISHLY DARK DEAL
Maggie Cox

THE COP, THE PUPPY AND ME
Cara Colter

BACK IN THE SOLDIER'S ARMS
Soraya Lane

MISS PRIM AND THE BILLIONAIRE
Lucy Gordon

DANCING WITH DANGER
Fiona Harper

0512 Rom LP